Gallery Books
Editor: Peter Fallon

HATCHET

Heno Magee

Hatchet

Heno Magee

Gallery Books

Hatchet is published simultaneously in paperback and in a cloth-
bound, limited edition of 200 copies signed by the author,
by
The Gallery Press
19 Oakdown Road
Dublin 14. Ireland.

© Heno Magee. 1978.

ISBN 0 902996 63 0 (*clothbound*)
0 902996 67 3 (*paperback*)

The Gallery Press gratefully acknowledges the assistance of An
Chomhairle Ealaíon (The Arts Council of Ireland) towards the
publication of this book.

Applications for a licence to perform this play by Professional or
Amateur Companies must be made in advance to the Gallery Press.

Hatchet

A PLAY IN THREE ACTS

The action of the play takes place in 1970, in the Bailey household—an artisan dwelling—and workingclass environs, including a lane at the rear of the dwelling; also, in and around Corrigan's Public House, set in the same locality.

Act I
THE BAILEY HOUSEHOLD
Time: Friday 12.30 p.m. approximately. Late Summertime.

Act 2
CORRIGAN'S PUBLIC HOUSE, AND SURROUNDS
Time: 10.30 p.m. approximately. The same day.

Act 3
THE BAILEY HOUSEHOLD AND BACK LANE
Time: About 10 a.m. The next day.

Hatchet was first produced at the Peacock Theatre, Dublin, on July 27th, 1972, with the following cast:

Angela Turner	Máire O'Neill
Bridie Bailey	Terri Donnelly
Ha Ha	Eamon Kelly
Mrs. Bailey	May Cluskey
Hatchet Bailey	John Kavanagh
Joey	Arthur O'Sullivan
Hairoil	Joe Dowling
Freddie	Robert Carlile
Workman	Michael Duffy
Barman	Michael Duffy
Barney Mulally	Bryan Murray
1st Policeman	Micheál O Briain
2nd Policeman	John Olohan
Johnnyboy Mulally	Donal Neligan
1st Man	Noel O'Donovan
2nd Man	Fergus O'Neill
Direction	Roland Jaquarello
Design	Brian Collins
Lighting	Tony Wakefield

Characters

Ha Ha, brother to Mrs Bailey, a bachelor, aged about 60 years
Mrs Bailey, a widow, about 55
Hatchet, her son, a docker, about 26
Bridie, his wife, about 23
Angela, her sister, a housewife, about 28*
Joey, a factory chargehand, on holidays from England, about 60
Hairoil, friend of Hatchet, about 26*
Freddie, friend of Hatchet, about 28
Workman, an electrician, about 40
Barman, rural character, about 50*
Barney Mulally, a petty thief, about 24
Johnnyboy, his brother, a psychopathic criminal and pimp, about 30
1st Man, }
2nd Man   } young toughs, ganglings of Johnnyboy, about 20
1st Policeman, rural character, about 35*
2nd Policeman, rural character, about 24*

Time and place:
Summer 1970, a tough workingclass area of Dublin, Ireland.

Notes: Angela should wear spectacles of a conservative design.
Hairoil should wear some type of headgear to conceal the
skin ailment that has made him prematurely bald. Both
policemen and barman should speak with a provincial
accent to give contrast and balance to the play.

Glossary

Oulwan	Old One, usually Mother
Oufella	Old Fellow, usually Father
Youngwan	Young One, usually Young Girl
Brasser	Prostitute
Slag	Corner Boy
Slagging	Jeering
Coddle	Dublin Soup (Bacon, Potatoes, Onions)
Burst	To burst a person . . . To beat a person up
Hardman	Tough Guy
Hardchaw	Aspiring tough guy, also Corner Boy

ACT ONE

SCENE. *The living room of the Bailey household, which consists of a backwall, with door top right, leading to Mrs Bailey's bedroom, which should be, at least, partially visible. The door, bottom of right side wall, leads to kitchen—and back yard (Pigeon loft). Most of the furnishing is old-fashioned, except a table and four chairs centre. The fireplace centre of left sidewall, with fireside chair, down. An old-fashioned sofa is top of fireplace. An old dresser is set at back wall, with T.V. set to the left of it. An old china cabinet is centre of right side wall.*

TIME. FRIDAY. 12.30 p.m. approximately. *In the late Summertime. When the curtain rises—We see Mrs Bailey awakening, groggily, in her bed. At the same time, in living room,* BRIDIE *is setting table for dinner.* ANGELA *is sitting on chair top right of table.* HA HA *is sitting on fireside chair rolling a cigarette.*

ANGELA   Did ye hear her last night, singing her head off?
BRIDIE   Hatchet had to go out and bring her in.
MRS B.   Jaysus. (*Scratching head*).
HA HA   Aha, aha, it's all going through life.
ANGELA   Baby was awake all night over her.
BRIDIE   The whole street was woken up.
MRS B.   God, what happened?
ANGELA   I don't know how you've stuck it this long, I swear.
BRIDIE   Get used to it, anyway he won't move, not yet.
MRS B.   BASTARD!
ANGELA   You're too soft, should put your foot down.
HA HA   Sez you, aha, aha.
BRIDIE   I wonder.
MRS B.   What did I do . . . yis?
ANGELA   Ye got a bad match, Bridie, and ye could've had your pick of fellas.
BRIDIE   Oh, what does it matter?
ANGELA   Look at me, moving into a private house on Monday, and you could've done as well.
HA HA   Aha, aha, sez you to her.
BRIDIE   Maybe.
MRS B.   God, shouldn't've done that, should've kept me head, yeah.
ANGELA   Could've had a lovely home, maybe children and all.

BRIDIE	How do you know? Look, don't keep going on about it. These things take time. Anyway, I'm only married a year, it's me first anniversary, not me twentieth, Angela.
ANGELA	Oh, I didn't mean anything by it. Bridie, did he get ye anything?
BRIDIE	I don't know yet.
MRS B.	Go way, ye impertinent pup. Barman, put him out.
ANGELA	Huh, you'll be lucky.
BRIDIE	Tch, you don't know him, Angela.
ANGELA	Not half.
BRIDIE	Ah stop, Angela, don't keep running him down.
MRS B.	(*dressing, looking in mirror*) Oh, me eye, the swine, bleedin' swine, glad now, should've shoved the glass and all into his face. Am I barred, am I?
ANGELA	Don't like the way he carries on, that's all.
BRIDIE	I know.
ANGELA	You'd think he was Clark Hudson, the way he swings them shoulders of his.
HA HA	Aha, Aha, aha, aha,
BRIDIE	It's just his way.
MRS B.	No, what was it now, yis, he didn't bar me, yis, last chance, that's it, yeah.
ANGELA	Miss ye all the same, Bridie, you'll come out and visit me?
HA HA	Me, me, me, me, aha, aha.
BRIDIE	Of course. I'll miss the children, ye gave them the presents?
ANGELA	Oh, they loved them. (*To* HA HA) You stop that you.
MRS B.	Pox bottle bastard, Hatchet will fix him, he'll get him, Jaysus, I wish it never happened, oh I miss ye, Digger, miss ye.
BRIDIE	Your children, Angela, did they just happen, or . . . er, did ye sort of, er, plan them?
ANGELA	Oh the first one there was no stopping, he came on his own, but, we spaced our other two.
BRIDIE	I see.
ANGELA	Why, is there anything happening?
BRIDIE	No, I just wondered.
ANGELA	You're sure you're not expecting?
HA HA	Ting, ting, ting, ting.
BRIDIE	Double sure.
ANGELA	(*to* HA HA) You stop that, what's he keep staring

	at me for?
HA HA	Aha, aha, for, for, for, for.
ANGELA	Should be in a home . . . ye madman.

Enter MRS BAILEY.

MRS B.	He is not mad, just a bit touched, that's all.
HA HA	Touch wood, aha, aha.
MRS B.	How would you be if you were beaten up selling a few paper hats?
ANGELA	What's he keep staring at me like that for?
MRS B.	Don't jeer my brother now, that's only melanjoysis.
HA HA	Ignition in your adam's apple.
MRS B.	Is Hatchet in?
BRIDIE	He's gone down the docks for his wages, be back soon, the dinner's just ready.
MRS B.	Cigarette, have ye a cigarette, Bridie?
BRIDIE	Sorry, gave the last one to Hatchet.
MRS B.	Have you . . . er?
ANGELA	I don't smoke, Missus.
MRS B.	'Course not.
HA HA	Will I go the shop, Nellie?
MRS B.	It's alright, Ha Ha, should be some in me handbag.

MRS B. *is moving to kitchen.*

BRIDIE	Angela's moving into her new house on Monday.
MRS B.	Is she? Oh good luck to ye, Angela, (*enters kitchen*) yis, ye stuck up bitch. (*Searches handbag for cigarette*).
ANGELA	See her eye? God only knows what she was up to last night.
BRIDIE	Ah, she probably only fell, Angela.
ANGELA	Yeah, fell by the wayside, ye mean.

Enters MRS B. *from kitchen.*

MRS B.	Yis, good luck to ye, Angela, I'll miss ye.
ANGELA	Oh, I'll still be calling down, now and then, to see Bridie.
MRS B.	Well, we'll have something to look forward to so.
ANGELA	Sure I couldn't forget me little sister.
BRIDIE	You're welcome anytime. Angela, but I'm 23 and well able to look after meself.

MRS B.	So you're getting out, are ye? Ah well, ye might be better off.
ANGELA	I'm not complaining.
MRS B.	Be out of it meself one day. None of us live forever, and Bridie and Hatchet will have it all to themselves.
BRIDIE	What, what was that?
MRS B.	This place, Bridie, when I'm gone, the house is yours. I'm buying it out by the week.
BRIDIE	Oh no it's not, Mrs Bailey.
MRS B.	Why not, won't it save ye buying an expensive home?
BRIDIE	It doesn't matter, Hatchet and me have our own ideas.
MRS B.	Oh, and what's wrong with here?
BRIDIE	I didn't say there was anything wrong with it, did I?
MRS B.	It's a bit old-fashioned, I know, but I was going to get rid of that sofa, and ye wouldn't want that dresser either, I know how you youngwans feel.
BRIDIE	It's not that, we want our own place.
ANGELA	Ye can't blame her for that, Missus.
MRS B.	Sure don't I know, Bridie, but wouldn't it be a terrible pity to let this place go to waste.
BRIDIE	Maybe it would.
MRS B.	You're terrible silly, Bridie, sure they'll shove ye out to the country. Silly, terrible silly, ye are.
BRIDIE	It doesn't matter where we go. It's what we always intended.
HA HA	I like you, Bridie.
MRS B.	It's a bit rough around here, I know.
ANGELA	Ye can say that again.
MRS B.	Can I now, can I say that again now?
BRIDIE	For God's sake, it's nothing like that.
ANGELA	Bridie knows her own mind.
MRS B.	Does she, and who's talking to you anyway?
ANGELA	I'm only trying to explain, Missus.
MRS B.	No one asked ye, it's nothing to do with ye.
BRIDIE	Leave it, Angela.
ANGELA	My sister's quite right, Mrs Bailey.
MRS B.	She doesn't need your advice, keep out of it.
BRIDIE	Will yis forget about it? It doesn't matter what anyone sez, alright?
ANGELA	Quite right, Bridie.
BRIDIE	We can look after ourselves.
ANGELA	Quite, quite.

ITEMS ISSUED/RENEWED
FOR Mr Peter Williams
ON 24/07/13 13:15:30
AT Tallaght

09029966301006
Hatchet
Due 16/08/13
Hire £0.50

1 item(s) issued

MRS B.	Quite, quite . . . d'ye ever shut yer trap?
BRIDIe	Oh don't start again, say nothing, Angela.
ANGELA	A body can't speak their mind now, I suppose.
MRS B.	Ye had yer spoke, don't get yer knickers in a knot now.
ANGeLA	D'ye mind, Missus, there's no call for that.
BRIDIE	Can yis not drop it?
MRS B.	Keep quiet, for Jaysus' sake. Me head is jumping.
ANGELA	Surely ye don't expect my sister to put up with that?
BRIDIE	Forget it, Angela.
MRS B.	You're an aggravating nose-poker, and you've said enough.
ANGELA	I'll say what I please.
MRS B.	(standing up) You're getting on me wick.
ANGELA	She'd be mad to stay here.
MRS B.	Don't start slagging, I'm warning ye.

BRIDIE gets between ANGELA and MRS B.

BRIDIe	That's enough, Angela.
ANGELA	The sooner ye get away from her the better.
MRS B.	(picks up cup) Ye pig ye, I'll split ye, if ye go on.
HA HA	Don't, don't fight, don't.
BRIDIE	Stop, in the name of God.
ANGELA	I wouldn't tolerate that, Bridie.
BRIDIE	Shut up, Angela.
ANGELA	Disgusting carry on.
MRS B.	Ye specky eyed cow, don't jeer me, I warned ye.

Enter HATCHET from door to hall.

BRIDIE	Will yis stop? Hatchet, do something.

HATCHET pushes them apart roughly.

HATCHET	What's bleedin' goin on?
BRIDIE	They were arguing.
MRS B.	I didn't start it.
HATCHET	Shut up, over what?
ANGELA	Your mother threatened to split me.
MRS B.	That's all, I didn't even touch her.
BRIDIE	It was over the house.
MRS B.	I just want yis to have it, that's all.

BRIDIE   I told her we didn't want it, and Angela . . .
MRS B.   Had to poke her big red nose in, didn't ye?
ANGELA   I have nothing more to say.

MRS B. *sits down.*

HATCHET   Ah, shut up the lot of yis, I'm famished, where's me
           dinner, where's me dinner, Bridie?
BRIDIE   (*entering kitchen*) I'm getting it, I'm getting it.

HATCHET *sits on chair bottom left of table.*

HATCHET   (*to Angela*) Sit down you, sit down.
MRS B.   Yis, ye make the place look untidy.

ANGELA *sits down.*

HATCHET   When are ye going to get sense, Ma? Arguing over
           that and, Angela, it's nothing to do with you what
           goes on in this house, get it? Ye want to mind yer
           own business, alright?
ANGELA   I was only trying to explain what Bridie wants, that's
           all, Brendan.
HATCHET   It's nothing to bleedin' do with ye, ye were told.
ANGELA   I'm her sister now, Brendan.
HATCHET   Ah, where's me dinner? (*Shouting*).

BRIDIE *enters with dinner pot, from kitchen, and places
it on table.*

BRIDIE   Here, help yourselves, and let's have a bit of peace at
           the dinner, at least.
ANGELA   (*standing*) Er. . . . I'll be off.
BRIDIE   What, and what about your dinner?
ANGELA   I can get something in the chipper.
HATCHET   Sit down, ye came here for your grub, Bridie will
           look after ye.
BRIDIE   C'mon Angela, we've got plenty. I made a coddle.
MRS B.   Go on, sit down and get a load off your mind.
ANGELA   (*sitting*) They switched off the gas, we should've
           moved in yesterday, but the house wasn't ready.
MRS B.   Ye don't have to make excuses, we'd refuse a bit to
           eat to no one. What about your poor husband?

ANGELA	He's getting his in work.
MRS B.	And your poor kids?
ANGELA	They're with his mother.
HATCHET	Get stuck in then.
MRS B.	See ye got the bones, Bridie.
BRIDIT	I always get them for the coddle, Hatchet likes them.
MRS B.	(*sucking bone*) Delicious, you should try them, Angela, they're good for your complexion.
ANGELA	There's nothing wrong with my skin, Missus.
HA HA	Trick cyclist, but how can ye back pedal?
ANGELA	Very tasty, Bridie.
MRS B.	(*wiping fingers in table cloth*) You should come tomorrow, we're having high tea on a low table, pardon me fingers, Angela.
ANGELA	I'll be in my own home tomorrow, please God.
MRS B.	Oh, of course, did ye see me eye, Hatchet, see me eye?
HATCHET	What's wrong with ye?
MRS B.	Me eye, look, it's black.
HATCHET	What happened ye?
MRS B.	I was insulted in the pub last night.
HATCHET	Jaysus, not again?
MRS B.	Wasn't my fault now.
BRIDIE	Eat up, Hatchet.
HATCHET	Wasn't it, whose bleeding fault was it this time?
MRS B.	Barney Mulally, he's always slagging me.
BRIDIE	Don't let it go cold, Hatchet.
HATCHET	Slagging, slagging, ye got that over slagging?
MRS B.	Not just that, he went too far this time, but he got a pint over him.
HATCHET	Ah, finish your dinner, outa that.
MRS B.	He hit me, he did. The swine, should've shoved the glass and all into his mush.
HATCHET	What d'ye expect, ye didn't think he was just going to sit there and take it, did ye?
MRS B.	He called me a brasser. ME! I'm no prostitute, I'm not.
ANGELA	Hmmmm.
BRIDIE	Of course not, Mrs Bailey.
HATCHET	We know that, we know that.
MRS B.	Wasn't putting up with that. He tried to get me barred, told them not to serve me.
HATCHET	What pub was this?
MRS B.	Corrigan's, Hatchet, I was just sitting there, this man

	handing me a drink . . .
HATCHET	What man, what man?
MRS B.	A man, a man, Joey, an old friend of the Digger's on holidays from England, and Mulally called him me fancy man in front of everyone.
ANGELA	Indeed.
HATCHET	Huh, and what did he bleedin' say that for?
MRS B.	I don't know, a small drop of drink fell on him, that was all.
BRIDIE	Finish your dinner, Hatchet.
MRS B.	Nuttin', over nuttin', and that swine had to make a show of me over it.
HATCHET	Alright, alright, forget about it, I'll sort him bleeding out.
MRS B.	What does he think I am?
HATCHET	Ye told us, let us get on with the dinner, will ye?
ANGELA	Not bad, Bridie, bit caught in me teeth.
MRS B.	Well take them out. They're false, aren't they?
ANGELA	Missus!
BRIDIE	Are ye going back to work this afternoon?
HATCHET	No, all the ships are unloaded. Heavy going next week, over six ships due Monday alone.
MRS B.	The dirty cur, pass the salt, a skinny swine is all he is.
BRIDIE	(*passing salt*) Let him get on with his dinner, Mrs Bailey.
ANGELA	Yes, you've got thin, Brendan.
HATCHET	Ah shut up, the lot of yis, I told ye, I'll get him Ma, didn't I, what more do ye want, and what about this Joey fella, what did he do about it?
MRS B.	Joey's real quiet, he wouldn't hurt a fly, you'll see him when he calls.
HATCHET	Here?
MRS B.	Yis.
HATCHET	He's calling to see you?
MRS B.	Not just me, you as well. Him and the Digger was great pals. They grew up together.
HATCHET	I see.
MRS B.	He's just calling, that's all, you're very inquisitive.
HATCHET	Yeah, yeah, did ye look in on the pigeons, Bridie?
ANGELA	Pigeons, YUK!
BRIDIE	Oh I forgot, Hatchet.
HATCHET	Ah, Bridie, and I asked ye specially, ye know Bella is up the pole, I'm trying to get a racer out of her.

BRIDIE	It slipped me mind.
HATCHET	They need plenty of attention when they're like that, Bridie, ye have to be sort of tender, and treat them gentle, that right, Ma?
MRS B.	Oh yis, particularly in the breeding season, the Digger used to be up all night with them sometimes.
BRIDIE	I'm sorry, Hatchet.
HATCHET	Well did ye get the seed?
BRIDIE	Yeah, I put it out in the loft.
HATCHET	That's something. I'm going to Belfast tomorrow for the pigeon race.
BRIDIE	Smashing!
HATCHET	I'm thinking of entering Blackie, d'ye want to come?
BRIDIE	Terrific, and I can do some shopping.
HATCHET	Can get a good hen and cock, and try me hand at breeding.
BRIDIE	Stupendous, Hatchet.
HATCHET	Might be able to build up some good racing stock.
BRIDIE	That's a great idea.
ANGELA	My husband's taking up stamp collecting.
MRS B.	I'm not surprised.
HATCHET	Yeah, course you'd have to look after the loft while I'm at work, Bridie, feed them and that. Ha Ha will help ye.
HA HA	Aha, aha, aha.
BRIDIE	I'd like that, I really would.
MRS B.	It's easy, I'll show ye.
HATCHET	Ye might have to clean out the loft sometimes.
BRIDIE	So what?
ANGELA	Don't know how anyone goes near them.
HATCHET	It stinks to high heaven sometimes, they're dirty bleeder', I'm not joking ye.
BRIDIE	I wouldn't mind, Hatchet, honestly, a smashing idea.
ANGELA	Them birds spread diseases, so they do.
MRS B.	Is that right, well they're not the only things that spread diseases.
BRIDIE	It's still a smashing idea.
MRS B.	Don't mind her, Bridie, we had the best stock in Dublin one time. The fanciers came from everywhere to deal with us, right Hatchet?
HATCHET	Ye can say that again, Ma.
MRS B.	And the Digger couldn't even read or write.
HATCHET	That's a fact.

19

MRS B.	(*standing up*) There's one for ye, Angela, now, let's get cleaned up.
HATCHET	What's the rush?
MRS B.	Now ye don't want Joey to find the place untidy, d'ye?
HATCHET	Whaaaat?
BRIDIE	(*standing*) Your mother's right, Hatchet, won't take a minute.
ANGELA	Cleanliness is next to Godliness.
HATCHET	Huh, I think ye're going round the bleedin' bend, Ma.
HA HA	Will I get the brush, Nellie?
ANGELA	(*standing*) And I shall do the dishes.
MRS B.	It's alright, you're a guest.
ANGELA	(*collecting plates*) Oh no, I shall do my bit.
HATCHET	(*lighting cigarette*) You don't have to, ya know.
ANGELA	Ye don't have to tell me, Brendan.

MRS B. *and* BRIDIE *tidy room,* HA HA *sweeps floor,* ANGELA *journeys between livingroom and kitchen with tableware.*

HATCHET	(*opens shirt*) How long is your man staying, Ma?
MRS B.	Hard to say, just a visit, that's all.
ANGELA	Look at him—stretching out like Tarzan.
HATCHET	So what—your Ladyship?
ANGELA	(*pointedly*) There's the ashtray, Brendan.

ANGELA *exits to kitchen.*

HATCHET	What sort of an eejit married her?
HA HA	Will I sweep the rooms, Nellie?
MRS B.	Yis, Ha Ha, good boy.
HA HA	(*exiting door to hall*) Ha Ha will sweep the rooms.
HATCHET	I suppose you'll be going out with your man tonight, Ma, will ye?
MRS B.	Yis, Corrigan's, yous are to come as well.
HATCHET	Not me, I'll be seeing Freddie and Hairoil.
BRIDIE	Not tonight, Hatchet.
HATCHET	Sure, the big fight's on at the Stadium, you can stay with me mother.
BRIDIE	Ah, Hatchet.
HATCHET	Won't I see ye in the pub later.
MRS B.	Don't worry, Bridie, I'll look after ye. (*looks around*

	room) How does it look?
BRIDIE	(*adjusting tablecloth*) Now, that's better.
MRS B.	It'll have to do, must get ready, he should be here soon.
HATCHET	Ye what? Get a grip of yourself, you're running around like a youngwan.
MRS B.	What do ye mean? I'm not dead yet, ye know, I've still got me figure. (*exits door to hall-upstairs bedroom*).
BRIDIE	You're not going to the fight are ye?
HATCHET	I said I was, didn't I?
BRIDIE	But ye don't have to go, Hatchet.
HATCHET	Don't I always go to the big fights? Anyway, I already promised Freddie and Hairoil.
BRIDIE	I'm not going to the pub without ye.
HATCHET	I'll pick ye up when the fight's over so.
BRIDIE	Ye got drunk and everything, the last time ye were with them.
HATCHET	(*standing*) Don't worry, Brid, I'll make it up to ye, there'll be a sing song and all, in the pub after.
BRIDIE	Tch, Hatchet, I though ye were stronger, I really did, ye can't go running around with them all the time.
HATCHET	Freddie is only after getting out of nick, what else could I do?
BRIDIE	Ye know what they're like, they're always in trouble.
HATCHET	Nuttin' will happen, Bridie (*putting arms around Bridie*) I haven't been in a row in years, not a real one anyhow.
BRIDIE	What about Mulally?
HATCHET	What about him? He couldn't beat snow off a rope.
BRIDIE	Still trouble.
HATCHET	Mulally? I'll beat him with me cap.
BRIDIE	It's nuttin' to joke about.

They kiss.

BRIDIE	Keep away from him, Hatchet.
HATCHET	Don't mind him, Brid.

They kiss again.

BRIDIE	(*avoiding kiss*) I only got me hair done.
HATCHET	I won't mess it.
BRIDIE	Ah stop it, Angela's in there.

HATCHET	So what?
BRIDIE	No, Hatchet.
HATCHET	Well c'mon we'll go to our own room so.
BRIDIE	We can't, Ha Ha is sweeping it out.
HATCHET	Well I'll get him bleedin' out.
BRIDIE	No, no, Hatchet.
HATCHET	Why in God's name not?
BRIDIE	I just don't feel like it.
HATCHET	What's up with ye this time?
BRIDIE	Nuttin', nuttin'.
HATCHET	Well c'mon then.
BRIDIE	No, I don't feel like it, Hatchet.
HATCHET	What's bleedin' wrong now?
BRIDIE	Just control yourself, Hatchet.
HATCHET	Control meself, Jaysus, you turned out great, didn't ye?

HATCHET *sits, brooding, smokes a cigarette.*

BRIDIE	I can't help it if that's the way I feel.
HATCHET	I ought to give ye a bleedin' dig, that's what anyone else around here would do.
BRIDIE	Everything's going wrong, everything.
HATCHET	I'm mad to be putting up with ye, ye hardly let me near ye.
BRIDIE	I don't be well sometimes.
HATCHET	There's always something wrong with ye. And as for that one, that one gives me a pain in the arse.
BRIDIE	What one?
HATCHET	Your sister, (*shouts*) ANGELA, ANGELA.
ANGELA	(*pokes head out of kitchen*) You don't have to shout, Brendan.
HATCHET	I wasn't talking to you.
ANGELA	Well what are ye roaring me name for?
HATCHET	Mind your own bleedin' business.
BRIDIE	It's just between us, Angela.
HATCHET	That nose of yours is going to get ye into trouble one day, d'ye know that?
BRIDIE	Leave us, Angela.
HATCHET	WELL?
ANGELA	Oh, fair enough, Brendan. (*head disappears*).
HATCHET	Brendan, and that's another thing, she's the only one that calls me that around here.

BRIDIE	She doesn't like your nickname.
HATCHET	She doesn't like me ye mean, she wouldn't even come to the wedding.
BRIDIE	She was sick.
HATCHET	She wasn't sick, she's too fuckin' miserable to get sick.

Slight pause.

BRIDIE	Ye didn't give me me money, Hatchet.
HATCHET	(*throwing wage packet on table*) There.
BRIDIE	Thanks ... er ... don't feel bad about what happened, Hatchet.
HATCHET	Ah get stuffed, d'ye know what that means, get stuffed, right?

HATCHET *goes to pigeon loft, examines birds, fills seed box.* BRIDIE *takes small parcel from glass cabinet, follows* HATCHET.

BRIDIE	How's Bella?
HATCHET	She's coming along.
BRIDIE	(*handing parcel to* HATCHET) That's for you, Hatchet.
HATCHET	What is it?
BRIDIE	Open it and see.

HATCHET *opens parcel, takes out cigarette lighter.*

HATCHET	A present, thanks Bridie.
BRIDIE	And don't pawn it, like the last one I gave ye.
HATCHET	I wouldn't've hocked it only I needed a new set of darts, honest, Bridie.
BRIDIE	Nuttin' for Bridie? Ye forgot, didn't ye? And it's only our first year.
HATCHET	Did I?
BRIDIE	Ye must've.
HATCHET	I forgot, didn't I?
BRIDIE	That's the way it looks.
HATCHET	Jays, you don't think much of me, d'ye? Did ye look at the wages I gave ye?
BRIDIE	Not yet.
HATCHET	Well ye want to take a good bleedin' look 'cos there's an extra fiver in there, alright?
BRIDIE	I never thought you'd give me money, Hatchet.

23

HATCHET	It's for that fancy handbag ye wanted in that posh place. Ye didn't expect me to go into a woman's shop, did ye?
BRIDIE	Ah, I'm sorry, Hatchet, really I am.
HATCHET	I wouldn't mind but the way they stare at ye in them places, you'd think I was going to rob the bleedin' shop.
BRIDIE	What's going to happen us, Hatchet?
HATCHET	I don't know, do I?
BRIDIE	All the plans we had.
HATCHET	Yeah, yeah.
BRIDIE	We should've gone straight off when we got married.
HATCHET	On what, hadn't I got to pay for me Da's funeral?
BRIDIE	We'd've managed somehow.
HATCHET	Sure, and leave me Ma on her own just after I buried me father.
BRIDIE	We can't stay here for ever.
HATCHET	Ah, stop, stop outa that, and don't be annoying me.
BRIDIE	Things will never work out here, never, I don't care what ye say.
HATCHET	Don't be moaning, it's not that bad.
BRIDIE	We'd be better off on our own, if we were somewhere else, Hatchet, I know it, if only . . . if . . .
HATCHET	If, if . . . if me aunt had balls she'd be me uncle, wouldn't she? We're here, aren't we, don't be dreaming.
BRIDIE	Have to think of the future, Hatchet.
HATCHET	Well it's no use harping on it, you'll just have to make the best of it, won't ye?
BRIDIE	I suppose so . . . are we still going to Belfast tomorrow?
HATCHET	Yeah, why not?
BRIDIE	It'll be a change to get away, can I pick one of the birds you're buying?
HATCHET	Yeah, and if ye pick a cranky one with a big beak, we'll call it after your bleedin' sister, alright?

HATCHET *and* BRIDIE *re-enter livingroom, as Mrs B. is entering from door to hall, looking gaudily glamorous, tight mini-skirt etc.*

MRS B.	Did he come yet?
HATCHET	My Jaysus!

BRIDIE	No one called yet.
MRS B.	Is me slip showing?
BRIDIE	Ye look fine, Mrs Bailey.
MRS B.	(*to* HATCHET) Now you behave yourself when Joey calls.

HA HA *enters from door to hall with christening shawl over head.*

HA HA	Me Adam's apple.
BRIDIE	Take that off, Ha Ha, this instant.
HATCHET	What are ye getting excited about?
BRIDIE	I don't want anyone near my things.
HA HA	(*avoiding* BRIDIE) Aha aha, cloak, cloak.
MRS B.	He's only playing, Bridie.
BRIDIE	Doesn't matter, that's me mother's christening shawl.
HATCHET	Let her have it, it'll do for drying her feet.

BRIDIE *takes shawl off* HA HA.

BRIDIE	Don't you ever go into our room again.
HA HA	Cloak, hide, cloak.
MRS B.	He didn't mean anything, Bridie.

BRIDIE *sits, folds shawl.*

BRIDIE	That's our room, ours.
HA HA	Sorry, Bridie, sorry. (*sits on fireside chair*).
BRIDIE	Just keep away from our things, Ha Ha.
MRS B.	Sure Ha Ha always does the rooms.
BRIDIE	That room is where we live, Missus, it belongs to us.
MRS B.	He was only sweeping it, Bridie.
BRIDIE	I don't want anyone in there. We have our own life to live, and don't want anyone interfering. Just leave us alone, will ye?

Knocks are heard at door to hall.

MRS B.	That's him, wait, I'm not ready. (*taking wig off dresser*). How do I look? (*puts on wig*).
HATCHET	Like a brasser, what are ye wearing that for? People will think you're on the game or something.

MRS B.   Is that right, now?

HATCHET   Yis, and yiv more bleedin' rings than a gypsy.

MRS B.   Very complimentary, you are, show him in, Bridie.

BRIDIE exits door to hall.

HATCHET   Yeah, let's see what this one's like.

MRS B.   You be nice now, Hatchet, and don't be saying things like that.

Enter JOEY and BRIDIE from door to hall.

JOEY   Ah, Nellie, what a night. The dead arose and appeared to many.

MRS B.   Come in, precious, I was just telling them all about ye, sit down beside me, and get familiar, but not too familiar, ha, ha, ha.

JOEY and MRS B. sit on sofa.

JOEY   Me sweet Nellie, (*looks at* HATCHET) and that's the boy, you're Hatchet alright.

HATCHET   How are ye?

BRIDIE sits on chair bottom right of table.

JOEY   Yis, Hatchet, that's the Digger's boy alright, Nellie. Spittin' image of him.

MRS B.   Isn't he? Spittin', spittin', I told ye. D'ye remember Ha Ha?

JOEY   Do I remember? How are ye Ha Ha?

HA HA   Eh?

JOEY   How are ye, oul' son?

HA HA   That's what I'm trying to figure out. I don't know whether I'm in or out. Did ye ever feel like that?

JOEY   Oul Ha Ha, still the same. There's a few bob.

JOEY hands HA HA some money.

HA HA   It would confuse ye like. Sweets, Nellie, sweets.

HA HA exits door to hall.
Enter ANGELA from kitchen.

ANGELA	The kitchen's done for ye, Missus, thanks for the dinner, hello Mister.
JOEY	Miss.
ANGELA	See ye in Corrigan's tonight, Bridie.
BRIDIE	You're going to Corrigan's?
HATCHET	Wonders will never cease.
ANGELA	Celebrating leaving this place, aren't I?
BRIDIE	What about the children?
ANGELA	Oh me husband will look after them. Wouldn't let him drink.
HATCHET	(*sings*) "For he's a jolly good fellow, he's a jolly good fellow."
ANGELA	Anyway, someone has to keep an eye on me little sister, and that . . . un . . . tamed husband of hers.
MRS B.	Don't lose the run of yourself, Angela, you'll be smoking and all next, if you're not careful.
ANGELA	Oh good luck—and to you Mister. By the way, I like your wig.

ANGELA *exits door to hall.*

MRS B.	Bridie's sister, and I don't like the way she said that.
BRIDIE	She didn't mean anything.
MRS B.	She always means something, that one, but you like it, don't ye, Joey?
JOEY	I love it, Nellie, sure I love every bone in your corset.
MRS B.	Good oul' Joey, still the same after all these years.
JOEY	Ah, of course, . . . and the Digger's no longer with us, Nell.
MRS B.	Gone, he died on me, Joey, died on me.
JOEY	Me oul' mate.
HATCHET	Ye don't say.
MRS B.	Joey was best man at the wedding.
HATCHET	Yeah, are ye married yourself?
MRS B.	No, Joey's too sensible, but he likes the girls all the same.
JOEY	Well, why buy a cow if ye only want a pint of milk?
MRS B.	Ha, the one oul' Joey, it's a pity you're not home for good.
JOEY	Sure they can't do without me, I'm a foreman now ye know?
BRIDIE	Doing what?

JOEY	All sorts of things, it's one of the biggest factories in the midlands.
BRIDIE	Could ye get Hatchet a job?
JOEY	No bother. Money's good too, and ye needn't worry about digs. I've got a big place all to meself.
HATCHET	Hold on, who said I was going away?
BRIDIE	I'm only asking.
MRS B.	What would he want to go away for? Hasn't he a good job, and a good home here?
JOEY	Ye could do worse than stay with the Mammy, alright.
BRIDIE	It's only in case he did want to go. At least we'd have a place to go to.
MRS B.	Sure aren't all his friends here and all?
HATCHET	What are yis getting all steamed up about?
MRS B.	There y'are, Hatchet's like meself. Never leave the place we were reared in.
JOEY	Ye can't beat your own, Nell, that's a fact.
HATCHET	I didn't say I'd never go, Ma. Ye never know, I might feel like it sometime. I don't know what I'm going to do tomorrow or the next day, do I?
BRIDIE	And the money's good over there.
MRS B.	What brought this on? Ye never talked about going away before.
HATCHET	Look, we're only talking, I didn't say I was going, did I?
JOEY	No harm in talking, I suppose, Nell.
MRS B.	You started all this, Bridie. You're getting as bad as your sister, you are.
HATCHET	(*shouting*) Bridie started nuttin'.
MRS B.	Well don't start roaring now.
HATCHET	(*roaring*) I'm not bleedin' roaring.
MRS B.	Anyway, ye can do what ye like. Don't care what yis do, ye can go off for all I care.
JOEY	I'm not telling ye to go, Hatchet, don't rush into something ye could regret.
MRS B.	Now, you listen to Joey.
JOEY	The devil ye know is better than the devil ye don't know . . . er nothing personal, Nellie.

Enter FREDDIE *and* HAIROIL *from door to hall.*
Both lounge against backwall.

HAIROIL	Hello fans, it's happy time, Hairoil is here.
MRS B.	There y'are, Hairoil.
HAIROIL	There y'are, gorgeous, who's yer man?
MRS B.	Me oul' flame Joey, of course.
HAIROIL	Sorry, er, Joey, pal.
MRS B.	Out again, Freddie, how's the wife and kids?
FREDDIE	Still the same . . . moaning.
BRIDIE	How many have ye got?
HATCHET	Four.
FREDDIE	Correct, pal, four God forbids.
BRIDIE	God for what?
HATCHET	God forbids—kids.
HAIROIL	Heard ye had a run in with one of the Mulally's last night.
MRS B.	Yis, Hairoil, the Barney Fella.
JOEY	A lout, boys, picking on a woman.
HAIROIL	All of them Mulallys is a gang of rogues. Didn't his oul fella get the golden pencil off the labour exchange.
FREDDIE	The what?
HAIROIL	The golden pencil for signing the dole for 30 years without a break.
MRS B.	Wouldn't work in a fit.
BRIDIE	That type is best left alone.
HAIROIL	Oh Johnnyboy, the eldest is best left alone alright. He's a right wideboy, Freddie done time with him in England.
FREDDIE	He's a sharp man, right enough, he ran the bleedin' prison.
HAIROIL	Sharp, you'd want barbed wire in your pockets when he's around. He's got birds and all on the game.
FREDDIE	He's got medals for living on immoral earnings.
JOEY	A blackguard.
HAIROIL	That Barney fella is a headcase always breaking up his own gaff.
MRS B.	He lost his marbles, just like his oufella.
HAIROIL	The head shrinkers told his oulwan that he had too many personalities or something, she was delighted and she went around telling everyone her son had more personalities than anyone else.
FREDDIE	When are we getting him, Hatchet?
MRS B.	Bridie thinks we shouldn't do anything.
BRIDIE	Sure he's not all there.
FREDDIE	I'll bleedin' get him for ye, right?

29

HATCHET	It's nuttin' to do with you.
HAIROIL	If he slagged my oulwan, I'd dance on him.
JOEY	And why not?
FREDDIE	Ye have to, pal, shams like Mulally would sneak up behind ye when ye least expect it.
MRS B.	That's right, Freddie.
FREDDIE	'Cos there bleedin' scared.
HATCHET	So what?
HAIROIL	They're not the only ones.
FREDDIE	Well I'm not bleedin' scared, I'm afraid of no one. Just say the word, Hatchet.
HATCHET	I don't need ye.

Knocks are heard at door to hall, BRIDIE *exits.*

FREDDIE	Don't I know? But what if some of his mates interfere, they'll be a gang of them selling black market tickets at the stadium tonight.
HAIROIL	Mulally's no use on his own, there's more guts in a kipper.
HATCHET	That's their hard luck, isn't it?

Enter BRIDIE *from door to hall followed by workman.*

BRIDIE	He's from the electricity board.
WORKMAN	Good day, where's the mains, I have to cut ye off.
HATCHET	Ye have to what?
WORKMAN	Mrs Bailey live here?
MRS B.	No, Queen Elizabeth, who do you think?
HATCHET	Ye were right the first time, Mister.
WORKMAN	Well, you're three months behind with the bill, and it's my job to cut off your supply.
HATCHET	Is he right?
MRS B.	News to me.
WORKMAN	(*takes out reference*) Ah now, Mam, ye got plenty of notice, it's all down here.
FREDDIE	Them bleedin' places would rob ye.
HAIROIL	Yeah, ye wouldn't have a light with them, he, he, he.
HATCHET	(*stands, takes reference*) Shut bleedin' up, Hairoil, let's see that.
HAIROIL	(*indicates to* FREDDIE *that they should leave*) We'll scarper . . . er . . . Hatchet, going over the boozer, see ye later.

30

HATCHET	(*reading*) Yeah, O.K., O.K.
HAIROIL	Right, bring your darts.
JOEY	See ye tonight, boys.
FREDDIE	See ye, pal.
JOEY	(*as* FREDDIE *and* HAIROIL *are exiting*) Any friend of Nellie is a friend of Joey's

FREDDIE *and* HAIROIL *exit door to hall.*

BRIDIE	Is it true?
HATCHET	(*handing back reference*) It's true alright. The mains are in there. (WORKMAN *enters kitchen*) How did ye manage that? Now we've no bleedin' light.
MRS B.	I didn't think I was that far behind.
JOEY	These things happen.
HATCHET	Ye knew alright, ye heard the man.
MRS B.	I thought I could've fixed it up in time.
HATCHET	Three months, Jaysus, how did ye let it go that far?
MRS B.	I let it slip.
JOEY	It could happen a bishop, Nellie.
BRIDIE	I paid ye every week, Mrs Bailey.
HATCHET	Why didn't ye pay it?
MRS B.	I didn't mean to let it go that far.
HATCHET	And what did ye do with the money?
MRS B.	It just went.
HATCHET	Went bleedin' where?
MRS B.	I done a few horses now and then.
HATCHET	Ye what, are ye bleedin' mad?
MRS B.	It was something to do, and it passed the time.
JOEY	Don't worry about it, Nellie.

WORKMAN *enters from kitchen.*

WORKMAN	Sorry about that.
BRIDIE	When will we get the light back?
WORKMAN	When the bill is paid, Miss, and not before, I'm afraid.

Enter HA HA *from door to hall.*

HA HA	Hello, man, hello.
WORKMAN	Oh, hello.
HA HA	(*holds out paper bag*) Sweets, haha, sweets.
WORKMAN	Excuse me. (*exits hurriedly door to hall*).

HA HA *sits on fireside chair.*

BRIDIE   Why didn't ye tell us it was overdue?

MRS B.   Didn't want to worry yis, I thought I could've won it back.

JOEY   We all go through a bad spell.

MRS B.   I was often lucky, Joey, especially when the docket had odd numbers.

BRIDIE   And what about the rent, is that behind as well?

MRS B.   No, no, I wouldn't interfere with that, that's being paid off by the week, ye can check up on that.

HATCHET   I don't know what to make of ye, Ma, I don't, gambling and bleedin' everything.

MRS B.   I often won, and I don't know what you're giving out about, I couldn't've kept this place going only for it.

HATCHET   We know, we know.

MRS B.   Your father was only casual on the docks for years now, don't forget that, and it was me kept this place going.

HATCHET   Off again.

JOEY   She done her best now.

HATCHET   Jays, ye made a right show of the place, didn't she Joey, me mates here and all?

JOEY   C'mon we go for a drink, Nellie?

MRS B.   Don't be slagging me now. I'll get the money. If I've to sell every stick of furniture in the house I'll get it, and don't be acting ashamed of me either.

HATCHET   What's eating ye this time?

MRS B.   Slagging me over me wig.

HATCHET   Ah, will ye get lost, where's me darts?

HATCHET *looks for darts in dresser and glass cabinet.*
MRS B. *preparing to leave, takes coat off back of door.*

BRIDIE   Are ye still going to the fight?

HATCHET   Didn't I tell ye, I was?

BRIDIE   What if ye meet Mulally?

HATCHET   That's too bleedin' bad for him, isn't it?

BRIDIE   Try and keep away from him, Hatchet.

HATCHET   I don't know where he's going to be, do I?

MRS B.   I know.

BRIDIE   Ah, keep out of it, Mrs Bailey, if it wasn't for you, he wouldn't be in this trouble in the first place.

MRS B.	Me, what trouble?
BRIDIE	What d'ye think?
MRS B.	Trouble, taking up for his mother? Me and the Digger were respected around here, and only because we stood up for ourselves, Missy.
BRIDIE	Yis, with bottles.
JOEY	Tough times.
MRS B.	The Baileys were afraid of no one, that right son?
HATCHET	Yeah, yeah.
BRIDIE	It's no use talking to ye.
MRS B.	The Digger would fight anyone, and so would Hatchet, I never reared a gibber.
BRIDIE	Leave Hatchet out of it.
HATCHET	Will yis drop it, for God's sake?
JOEY	Are we going, Nell?
MRS B.	How d'ye think he got his name, for Jaysus' sake?
BRIDIE	I know.
MRS B.	Hadn't he to face the animal gang with a hatchet when he was only fourteen, didn't ye son?
HATCHET	What d'ye keep going on about it for?
JOEY	Yis, let bye-gones be bye-gones.
BRIDIE	You sent him down, Missus, he told me.
MRS B.	Of course, wasn't four of them kicking the head off his father.
HATCHET	Forget about it.
MRS B.	But he cleared them, screaming and roaring, there was a few skulls cracked that day, I'm telling ye.
BRIDIE	That was years ago.
HATCHET	Will ye bleedin' stop it, what d'ye keep bringing it up for?
MRS B.	Alright, son, forget about Mulally, don't mind me.
JOEY	C'mon, Nellie, a drink will do ye good.
HATCHET	I told ye I'll bleedin' get him, didn't I?
MRS B.	No, don't bother, do as your wife tells ye.
BRIDIE	He doesn't have to do anything for me, Missus, not like that anyhow.
MRS B.	Ah get off your high horse, who d'ye think ye are?
BRIDIE	I'm his wife, Missus.
HATCHET	Will yis stop bleedin' arguing?
MRS B.	Is that right? Alright, alright, yis have each other.
HATCHET	Stop it, I'll get that skinny pig, I'll break his bleedin' neck.
MRS B.	Are ye right, Joey? (*walking to door*).

JOEY   Right as rain, Nell.

MRS B.   (*at door*) Are ye coming with me, Ha Ha?

HA HA   (*stands up*) Aha aha. (MRS B. *and* JOEY *exit*) Am I coming sez you, or am I going sez I? It must be somewhere in between.

HA HA *exits door to hall.*

HATCHET   What are ye arguing with me mother for?

BRIDIE   She gets me going, Hatchet, I swear it.

HATCHET   Well I don't want to hear any more of it tonight, d'ye hear? Where's me darts?

BRIDIE   She has me as bad as herself, it's getting worse instead of better, she annoys me, I can't even think when she's around.

HATCHET   Ah, stop, stop, I'm not going to stand anymore of that, I'm telling ye, where's me darts? WHERE'S ME JAYSUS DARTS?

CURTAIN

END OF ACT ONE

Time—*10.30 p.m. the same day.*

Scene: *Corrigan's Public House, set in the same locality. In Pub—Bar is set against backwall—it is about three feet short of both side walls. The door to "Ladies" is up top against left sidewall. Set centre in left sidewall is a dartboard with light overhead, a "Dart Club" notice board is on one side with a "Marking Board" on the other side. The door to "Gents" is bottom left of side wall. There are approximately eight stools at bar. A small table is down centre with three chairs. A long cushioned bench is set against right side wall, which contains a plate glass window. Three small round tables with a stool each are set at bench. The entrance to pub is bottom of right side wall. A laneway winds right of Pub. As the curtain is rising characters walk to their places singing "Delilah".* MRS BAILEY *and* JOEY *are seated at table centre.* BRIDIE *and* ANGELA *are seated at table bottom of bench.* HATCHET *and* FREDDIE *play darts.* HAIROIL *marks board.* HA HA *is standing at bar. Extras may be used at the discretion of director.*

MRS B.   I saw the light, on the night, that I passed by her winda.
CHORUS   Da, da, da, da, da, da, da.
MRS B.   I saw the flickering shadows of love on her blind.
CHORUS   Da, da, da, da, da, da, da.
MRS B.   She was my woman, as she deceived me, I watched and went out of my mind. My, my, my Delilah.
CHORUS   Get them off ye.
MRS B.   Why, why, why Delilah?
CHORUS   Put them back on ye.
MRS B.   I could see that girl was no good for me, but I was lost like a slave that no man could free, at break of day when that man drove away, I was waiting.
CHORUS   Da, da, da, da, da, da, da.
MRS B.   I crossed the street to her house and she opened the door.
CHORUS   Da, da, da, da, da, da, da.
MRS B.   She stood there laughing.
CHORUS   Ha, ha, ha, ha, ha, ha, ha.
MRS B.   I felt the knife in my hand and she laughed no more. My, my my Delilah.
CHORUS   Get them off ye.
MRS B.   Why, why, why Delilah?

35

CHORUS	Put them back on ye.
MRS B.	So before they come to break down the door, forgive me Delilah, I just couldn't take anymore.

Applause, cheers etc.

HAIROIL	Very good, Mrs Bailey, I never knew ye couldn't sing.
JOEY	Lovely, Nellie, just like old times.

HATCHET *marks board for* FREDDIE *and* HAIROIL.

HATCHET	She's always mouthing.
ANGELA	So this is where he brings ye.
BRIDIE	Sometimes.
FREDDIE	(*throwing darts*) Am I away, Hairoil?
HAIROIL	Ye what? Ye wouldn't get away in a brothel.
FREDDIE	(*takes a swipe at* HAIROIL's *hat*) Get away ye scabby bleedin' head.
HAIROIL	(*Sparring and dodging* FREDDIE) Watch it, you're not in the Stadium now.
FREDDIE	Get up, the little bloke was a great goer, a real Cagney, he destroyed the English fella—like this.
HAIROIL	Bleedin' destroyed him, bup, bup.
MRS B.	(*encouraging*) Good on ye, Hairoil.
	FREDDIE *and* HAIROIL *enter a serious discussion on the merits of Cagney and Bogart.*
FREDDIE	Cagney was great, the way he went on, ye dirty no good bleedin' copper.
JOEY	Same again for my friends, barman, and a small one for Hatchet. (*Barman serves drinks*).
HAIROIL	Ah I preferred Humphrey, he handled the women better.
FREDDIE	What, did ye see Cagney in er . . . The Roaring Twenties? He was the head crook in it, he bleedin' milled everyone, right Hatchet?
HATCHET	Whatever you say, Freddie. Don't drink anymore, Bridie.
BRIDIE	Only lemonade.
HAIROIL	Ah, he wasn't as good as Humphrey . . . if ye don't mind me saying so, Hatchet.
ANGELA	The King is in his castle.
FREDDIE	Bogart was no use, pal, he had to use his gun all the time, Cagney had to only use his fists.

36

FREDDIE'S *temper is rising.*

HAIROIL So what? The way Humphrey chatted up Lauren, hello blue eyes.

FREDDIE (*grabbing* HAIROIL *by the throat*) That's no use, he was afraid to fight Cagney, he wouldn't even get in the same picture with him.

HAIROIL He *was* in a film with him.

FREDDIE He bleedin' wasn't, ask Hatchet.

HATCHET (*pushing them apart*) Cut out the messing.

HAIROIL (*going to bar*) Alright, Hatchet.

FREDDIE Nothing wrong with James, he was a real man.

HAIROIL (*to* HA HA) D'ye take a drink?

HA HA (*nodding*) Pink ink.

HAIROIL Well don't take mine or I'll bash ye.

Enter MULALLY *wearing cap and overcoat.*
BARMAN *comes out from behind bar.*

MRS B. Ah look who it is?

HAIROIL Don't kick that cap—there's a man under it.

BRIDIE *runs over to* HATCHET.

HATCHET It's alright, Bridie.

BARMAN Go on home, Mulally.

MULALLY I want a drink.

HAIROIL Ah, the baby wants his bottle.

BARMAN Ye have enough, come back tomorrow.

MULALLY I want one now.

FREDDIE Ye heard the man.

BARMAN You're getting nothing, you're barred.

MULALLY For what?

BARMAN I'm not serving ye, that's final.

MULALLY No, but you'll serve that brasser, won't ye?

HATCHET I'll bleedin' kill you.

BRIDIE Hatchet don't, please don't.

HATCHET Shut your bleedin' mouth, Mulally.

MULALLY *whips out saw.*

MULALLY Don't come chasing me, Hatchet, it was your oulwan started it, not me. (*hits saw off table—all stand*).

37

HATCHET	Get bleedin' out of here.
BRIDIE	No trouble, Hatchet, not tonight, please, for my sake.
FREDDIE	(*taking out razor*) You're for it, Mulally.
MULALLY	(*waving saw*) I'll give you this across the mush, and you, and you, and you.
HA HA	Aha, the truth, is it only a rumour, is it? Aha.
MULALLY	(*turning to* HA HA) Or any of yis!
BARMAN	Don't be foolish, put that away, the police will be around checking on closing time.
MULALLY	I'm not getting barred for nothing.
HAIROIL	Go home to your mammy.
FREDDIE	Heh, or one of your daddies.
MULALLY	I'll be here tomorrow with me brothers, and we'll see what happens then.
MRS B.	You'll get what's coming to ye.
BARMAN	Be a good man, now, I don't want to see ye going to prison.
MULLALY	I'm going, but I'm telling ye, you get your son to keep away from me.
MRS B.	Sparrowfart—my son's a man.
BARMAN	C'mon, c'mon now.
MULALLY	I'll take someone's life, if anyone comes after me again.
FREDDIE	Again and again and again.
MULALLY	I'm afraid of no one.
MRS B.	Go way, ye swine ye.
HATCHET	Get bleedin' moving. (*throws dart at* MULALLY'S *foot*).
FREDDIE	Quick. (*brandishing razor*).
HATCHET	(*taking razor off* FREDDIE) Take it easy, Freddie.
BARMAN	Let him go.
MULALLY	(*exiting*) Don't bleedin' come after me, I'm warning ye.

MULALLY *exits, runs up laneway,* FREDDIE *follows.*

FREDDIE	(*shouting up laneway*) We'll get ye, ye bastard.
HA HA	I wish I was an apple on a tree, but would that help ye?

BARMAN *goes behind bar,* FREDDIE *re-enters bar.*

ANGELA	I knew there'd be trouble.
MRS B.	Is he gone?

HATCHET	We know where to find him.
FREDDIE	Yeah, he went in the singing house.
ANGELA	(*at* HATCHET) Look at him—should be in a cage.
MRS B.	What's he always jeering me for?
JOEY	Don't mind him, Nellie.
MRS B.	Jaysus, over a year ago he wouldn't dared say that to me. The Digger would've thrown him through the winda, saw or no saw.
JOEY	Ah now, sure you've still got Hatchet.
FREDDIE	I was going to jump him only for that saw.

HATCHET *and* BRIDIE *go to bar.*

HATCHET	Ye shouldn't have got in me way, Bridie.
BRIDIE	Leave it Hatchet, it's over.
MRS B.	Swine, doesn't pick on anyone else, bleedin' swine.
FREDDIE	Don't worry, he'll be bleedin' bottled.
HAIROIL	Correct.

HAIROIL *and* FREDDIE *play darts.*

JOEY	Forget all about him, Nellie, get that drink down ye, (*hands her envelope*) and take care of that.
MRS B.	I couldn't, Joey.
JOEY	Take it now, we've known each other a long time, me oul' flower.
MRS B.	This is only a loan, Joey, you'll get it back, I swear to God on that.
JOEY	Don't you worry about that, Nellie.
MRS B.	(*kissing* JOEY) You're a good friend, Joey, one of the best.
HATCHET	Look at her, will ye behave yourself.
MRS B.	Ah, sour puss, Mulally has him annoyed.
HATCHET	Is that right?
MRS B.	Yis, it's not my fault now, I didn't say anything to him. Did I, Joey?
JOEY	Not a dickie bird.
HAIROIL	He's lucky he had that saw.
JOEY	No one could do anything about that.
FREDDIE	Let's get him now.
HATCHET	Take your time, I've hardly had a drink yet.
BARMAN	No trouble here, Hatchet, or I'll bar the lot of yis, your mother included.

HATCHET	He won't be done here, relax outa that.
BARMAN	And yous two are lucky to be served at all.
HAIROIL	In that case we'll come here often no more.
FREDDIE	Except when we want to.
ANGELA	Don't you get involved, Bridie.
MRS B.	Ah, the Mother Superior speaks from the diddy parlour.
FREDDIE	The bleeder deserves a hiding.
HAIROIL	His card's marked, isn't it?
HATCHET	For Jaysus sake, I came over for a drink with me wife, that's all, O.K.? You're too eager for a row, Freddie, give us the board, Mick.

BARMAN *gives* HATCHET *board, writes down names of dart team.*

FREDDIE	Ye have to look after yourself, pal.
HAIROIL	It's only natural.
FREDDIE	My father and mother was always at it.
HAIROIL	They were married, weren't they?
FREDDIE	'Course, me oufella used to rob the gas meter, and I'd get milled over it. He wouldn't bleedin' do it now.
HA HA	Aha, aha, ha, ha, why is the ceiling looking down on the floor?
FREDDIE	And it was him that got me married, he told a judge if he let me off I'd settle down and join the B.A.
HAIROIL	Ye were lucky ye didn't get a stretch.
FREDDIE	I wasn't me arse lucky, me mot was up the stick and I didn't know it.
HAIROIL	Women! I told my missus if she'd been born in India, she would've been worshipped.
FREDDIE	They do quare things in them places.
HAIROIL	She was delighted till she found out they worshipped cows over there.

HATCHET *puts down dart board.*

HATCHET	You're playing on Monday, Hairoil, and don't let us down like ye did the last time.
HAIROIL	'Nuff sed.
HATCHET	This is an important match, we want everyone there by half-eight.
HAIROIL	The job's right, skipper, say no more.

HATCHET	And you're one of the subs, Freddie.
FREDDIE	Not a Jaysus gain.
MRS B.	Sing a song someone, it's like a wake in here.
HATCHET	Will ye shut up outa that.
ANGELA	(*to Bridie*) Where's the . . . er?
BRIDIE	Over there. (*points to Ladies*).

FREDDIE *and* HAIROIL *sing "We know where you're going"*.

ANGELA	How dare ye! (*enters Ladies*).
HAIROIL	Did ye ever wake up in the morning and look under the bed to see if ye lost any sleep?

FREDDIE *and* HAIROIL *play darts*.

MRS B.	Give them a drink, barman, (*shouts*) here are ye deaf or something?
HATCHET	Don't be roaring.
MRS B.	I called for a drink and he won't even look at me.
JOEY	Barman, the lady wants ye.
BARMAN	What is it?
MRS B.	A drink, what else? Ye don't think I'm waiting on a bus, d'ye?
HATCHET	Keep quiet, you're making a show of yourself.
MRS B.	Ah, sorry Hatchet, sorry Bridie.
BRIDIE	It's alright.
JOEY	You're doing fine, Nell.
HA HA	Did ye ever get fog in your ears?
BARMAN	(*giving him a drink*) No, Ha Ha, no.
HA HA	Aha, it would make ye think when ye drink.

Enter ANGELA *from Ladies*.
HAIROIL *and* FREDDIE *sing "We know where ye've been"*.

MRS B.	Mind Freddie doesn't give ye a dart, Angela.
HAIROIL	(*Slapping* ANGELA *on rear*) How are ye, sexy?
ANGELA	Do yis mind, yis ignorant wasters?
FREDDIE	Well meself, I don't, I'm intoxicated with the exhuberance of me own ignorance.
ANGELA	(*sitting*) Ah, get a job for yourselves.

FREDDIE *and* HAIROIL *sing "We are the boys from the Summerhill, we never worked, and we never will".*

JOEY	Fair play lads.
ANGELA	Yis ought to be ashamed of yourselves.
HAIROIL	Don't worry, Angela, something will turn up.
FREDDIE	One bleedin' way or the other.
HAIROIL	Just like Adolf used to say "God never closed one gas oven, but he opened another".
MRS B.	(*singing*) Everyone is beautiful in their own way.
HATCHET	What are ye singing your head off for?
MRS B.	Well, it's better than thinking, isn't it? What's wrong with ye? (*salutes* JOEY *with her drink*) Bottoms up Joey, yaa hoo.
JOEY	Well said, Nellie.
HATCHET	Jaysus.
MRS B.	How are ye, Angela?
ANGELA	I'm fine, thank God.
MRS B.	Ye know Angela, Joey.
JOEY	A grand girl.
MRS B.	She's real holy.
ANGELA	I do my duty, Missus.
MRS B.	She's a secret agent for the legion of Mary, she washes her drawers in holy water, ha, ha, ha.
ANGELA	Ye should bless yourself, Mrs Bailey.
HA HA	(*stirring pint with finger*) Strawberries and scream?
MRS B.	(*going over to* HATCHET) C'mere, Joey, c'mon over love.

JOEY *goes over to* MRS BAILEY.

JOEY	**Yis** me oul' cabbage?
MRS B.	Tell them what ye done.
JOEY	Now that was just between you and me Nellie.
HATCHET	What did he do?
MRS B.	You tell them . . . alright, Joey is looking after the light bill.
HATCHET	Is he now?
JOEY	Ye shouldn't 've mentioned it.
MRS B.	Why not, and I didn't even ask him, did I Joey?
JOEY	Sure ye didn't have to, Nellie.
MRS B.	He made me take it.
HATCHET	Is that right?

BRIDIE	That was very good of ye.
JOEY	It was nothing, forget about it.
HATCHET	Oh sure.

JOEY returns to seat.

MRS B.	I will not forget about it.
HATCHET	He paying it all?
MRS B.	Yis.
HATCHET	Why?
MRS B.	Joey and me is old friends.
HATCHET	As long as he doesn't expect something back for it.
MRS B.	Don't be like that now, you should be grateful, anyway it's all fixed up, and there's no more reason for us to fall out, alright Hatchet, Bridie?
BRIDIE	It's alright as long as it doesn't happen again.
MRS B.	Don't worry love, I'm finished backing anyway.
BRIDIE	I hope so, Mrs Bailey.
MRS B.	Ye needn't fear, you can look after the light, the rent and things like that from now on.
BRIDIE	If ye like.
MRS B.	Sure it's your house really, I told ye that, now, that's finished, right?
BRIDIE	Whatever ye say.
MRS B.	Lovely, friends again, no more arguments and talk about going away and things. O.K.? We're a family (*shouts*) one big happy family.
HATCHET	Don't be shouting.
MRS B.	Together again. (*Sings her version of "The green, green grass of home"*) The old home town looks the same, as I step down from the train, and there to greet me is . . . er Hatchet and Joey, down the road I look and there runs me Bridie, hair of da, de, da, de, dady, . . . I forget, c'mon, sing someone.
JOEY	Lovely Nellie, like a bird.
HATCHET	What a bleedin' carry on.
MRS B.	Sing Angela, you're getting out aren't ye?
ANGELA	Thank God.

MRS BAILEY *sings "Bouna Sera". Most of the characters join in with the chorus.*

MRS B.	Bouna Sera, Signorina, Bouna Sera, it is time to say good night to Napoli, though it's hard for us to whisper, Bouna Sera, with that old moon above the Mediterranean Sea, in the morning, Signorina, we'll go walking, where the mountains and the sand come into sight, by the little jeweller's shop, we'll stop and linger, while I buy a little ring for your finger.
CHORUS	Your big fat finger, your big fat finger.
MRS B.	In the meantime, let me tell you that I love you, Bouna Sera, Signorina, kiss me goodnight.

Cheers, applause etc. MRS B. *pulls* JOEY *out of seat.*

MRS B.	C'mon handsome, give us a song.
HATCHET	Leave him alone.
JOEY	Ah, Nellie, ye know I can't sing.
MRS B.	Me lovely Joey, the man I dyed me hair for, what about the song ye got six months for? All the girls in France, Take their knicker down and dance, Singing Nellie put your belly Close to mine.

MRS B. *kisses* JOEY.

HATCHET	Will ye stop messing?
MRS B.	Go way with ye.
HATCHET	(*to* JOEY) And you stop hanging out of her, d'ye hear?
MRS B.	I love Joey.
HATCHET	(*pushing her away*) Get away from him and take that stupid bleedin' thing off ye. (*grabs wig and throws it on floor*).

MRS B. *picks up wig and sits down at table.*

MRS B.	What's wrong with you? Can I not enjoy meself?
HATCHET	You're making a bleedin' show of yourself.
MRS B.	You're too contrary, you are.
JOEY	Don't be like that, Hatchet, only having a bit of fun.
HATCHET	What's it got to with you, are you a bleedin' fancy man or something?

JOEY	ME?
ANGELA	Look at him.
BRIDIE	Hatchet.
HAIROIL	Nothing to sweat about, Bridie.
HATCHET	If I thought ye were I'd bleedin' bust ye here and now.
JOEY	I done nothing, Hatchet.
FREDDIE	Trouble pal?
MRS B.	Leave Joey alone now.
HATCHET	You shut up, and you're not married, how's that?
JOEY	Er . . . er . . . sure I'm a bachelor.
BRIDIE	You're being awkward, Hatchet.
ANGELA	Let him fight.
MRS B.	That's personal, don't mind him, Joey.
JOEY	I just didn't get round to er . . .
HATCHET	Ye just didn't, a big hard man like you. Plenty of readies, plenty of oul chat, and ye didn't, huh? But ye were hanging out of me mother fast enough, weren't ye?
JOEY	Being friendly, Hatchet.
MRS B.	Stop that now, Joey's one of our own.
HATCHET	He's a stranger to me. I don't know him, and I don't want him messing with you again, or I'll bleedin' do him, alright?
FREDDIE	Absobleedinlutely.
BRIDIE	Stop it, Hatchet.
HATCHET	Are you chasing me mother . . . well are ye going to answer?
HAIROIL	Answer the man.
JOEY	Me chasing? Ah Hatchet.
BRIDIE	Joey didn't do anything.
JOEY	I don't know why you're picking on me, Hatchet, I'm not a hard man.
ANGELA	He's civilised.
HATCHET	Is that right?
JOEY	Nellie will tell ye that.
MRS B.	There's nuttin' wrong with Joey.
JOEY	I'm no fancyman either, Nellie and me are oul pals, trying to have a bit of fun, that's all.
MRS B.	Now you apologise, Hatchet, apologise to Joey.
ANGELA	Him?
HATCHET	Ya what, I'm apologising to nobody.
BRIDIE	Just say you're sorry.
ANGELA	He doesn't know what it means.

45

HATCHET	But I'm not bleedin' sorry.
FREDDIE	Why should he be?
JOEY	It doesn't really matter.
HAIROIL	Let the hair sit.
MRS B.	It does matter, you do the right thing now.
HATCHET	If I do you'll bleedin' regret it, I'll turn this shop inside out.
MRS B.	Joey's A.1, a fine one you are, picking on me friends, is that the way I brought ye up, is it?
HATCHET	Is that the way ye brought me up? Don't start that, I'm telling ye.
BRIDIE	Leave it, Hatchet.
HATCHET	Tell him why I'm checking up on him.
MRS B.	Oh just a minute, hold your horses, what do ye mean by that?
HATCHET	Ye know, what the row was over, what Mulally called ye.
MRS B.	He knows, Joey knows, he was here when it happened.
JOEY	It wasn't Nellie's fault.
HATCHET	Was he now, and does he know why that bastarding pig called ye a prostitute, does he?
MRS B.	I don't know what you're getting at.
HATCHET	No ye don't, you're only over here every night getting gargled with someone, did ye tell him that?

HAIROIL *indicates to* FREDDIE *that they should keep out of a family dispute, they play darts keeping a watchful eye on events.*

MRS B.	So that's what's eating ye, well I'll tell him.
JOEY	Ah sure there's no need for that, Nell.
HATCHET	Well tell him.
MRS B.	I'm telling him, gimme a chance. A lot of people buy me drink, what's wrong with that? But they get nuttin' for it, Joey. Feck-all. And you know that, Hatchet.
JOEY	Sure, sure.
HATCHET	And why are they throwing the booze into ye, because ye look undernourished?
MRS B.	They're friendly, that's all, we get on well together.
JOEY	Of course.
HATCHET	Who are ye kidding? Them bleeders aren't throwing the gargle into ye just to hear ye nattering.

46

MRS B.	Maybe not, but I do nuttin' wrong.
HATCHET	No.
MRS B.	I take their drink alright. Yis. And listen to their dirty jokes. And tell a few too, doesn't bother Nellie, they think they're on to a good thing. But they do have another think coming I'm telling ye.
JOEY	No better woman.
MRS B.	What d'ye want me to do? I'm fed up in that room so I am, sitting and reading the wallpaper and counting me toe nails everyday. Browned off with it. I can't reach you anymore. And Bridie and her sister look down their nose at me so they do.
BRIDIE	It's not like that, Mrs Bailey.
ANGELA	And I do no such thing.
MRS B.	Ya do, ya do, ya do, ya do, . . . at least there's a bit of life over here. It's better than been stuck in like a statue anyhow . . . and me own son, Joey, is throwing that up into me face.
JOEY	Ye don't have to explain, Nell, ye done nothing to be ashamed of.
MRS B.	Not to you, I don't.
HATCHET	It's your own fault. Ye asked for it. What do ye act the bleedin' whore for?
JOEY	Ah now, none of that.
MRS B.	What's that ye said?
HATCHET	Ye heard me. Carrying on like a whore. What d'ye expect people to think?
MRS B.	Jaysus! I took it from Mulally (*throws pint into* HATCHET's *face*) but I won't take it from me own.
HATCHET	Ye rotten oul cow!

JOEY *and* BRIDIE *intervene.* BRIDIE *leads* HATCHET *to bar.*

JOEY	Sit down, sit down.
BRIDIE	(*wiping* HATCHET's *clothes with a hankie*) Don't mind her. C'mon we go home.
HATCHET	I'm not going bleedin' anywhere.
MRS B.	He's in his huffs, don't mind him, give him a drink.
HATCHET	Stuff your drink.
MRS B.	That's lovely, isn't it? I'm your mother, don't forget.
HATCHET	I know, Jaysus I know, are yis with me?
HAIROIL	Say the word, pal.
FREDDIE	What are we bleedin' waiting for?

BRIDIE	Don't go, Hatchet.
HATCHET	You stay with your dear sister.
ANGELA	Let him go.
HATCHET	Are yis right? (*making his way to pub entrance*).
FREDDIE	Does a cat drink milk?
HAIROIL	Right skipper.

HATCHET, FREDDIE *and* HAIROIL *go outside pub, and stand on footpath.*

FREDDIE	We after Mulally?
HATCHET	If he's not too gargled.
HAIROIL	Supposing he doesn't come this way?
FREDDIE	He has to. Doesn't he live down there? Anyway if we don't get him we'll get bleedin' someone.
HAIROIL	I'll see if the rat's still in his hole.

HAIROIL *exits down laneway.*

HA HA	(*About to light a cigarette*) Going to burn ye, Willie, the heat treatment, what's that got to do with a hen's egg, but.
BARMAN	Time up now please, think of the law, and I don't mean your mother in law.
ANGELA	Time for beddy byes, Bridie.
HAIROIL	(*Singing down lane*) My wife's a cow, my wife's a cow, my wife's a cowkeeper's daughter.
FREDDIE	(*shouting*) Shut up ye mouth.
HAIROIL	She loves her ol', she loves her ol' she loves her old Johnny Walker.
FREDDIE	Shut up, Hairoil, you'll get us bleedin' lagged.
HAIROIL	I've seen her as, I've seen her as,

Enter two uniformed policemen from left wing.

HAIROIL	I've seen her ask for more.

Enter HAIROIL *from laneway.*

1st P. MAN	What were ye doing down there?
HAIROIL	I was having a slash, why? Are you in charge of slashing around here?

2nd P. MAN	A funny man.
1st P. MAN	What are you doing here in the first place?
FREDDIE	We always hang around here.
HAIROIL	Yeah, except when we're somewhere else.
1st P. MAN	Stand up there together and let's see.
2nd P. MAN	Search them.

2nd P. MAN *starts to search* HAIROIL.

FREDDIE	What's all this about, we done nuttin' pal.
1st P. MAN	We'll see about that.
HAIROIL	Here, don't make a career of it down there, ye could be left like that.

2nd POLICEMAN *goes on to* FREDDIE.

FREDDIE	You're wasting your bleedin' time.

2nd POLICEMAN *goes on to* HATCHET, *discovers razor in inside pocket.*

2nd P. MAN	What's this now?
HAIROIL	It's a razor.
2nd P. MAN.	Is it now, and what are you doing with it?
HATCHET	What's the difference, it's only a razor.
1st P. MAN	It's an offensive weapon.
2nd P. MAN	And it'll get you six months.
HATCHET	For what? I didn't use it on anyone.
2nd P. MAN	You shouldn't be carrying it.
1st P. MAN	We're pulling you in.
HATCHET	You're not pulling me bleedin' in.
2nd P. MAN	Now don't give us any trouble.

HA HA, BRIDIE, ANGELA, JOEY *and* MRS BAILEY *leave pub. Two* POLICEMEN *approach either side of* HATCHET.

1st P. MAN	Now don't interfere, lads.
FREDDIE	He done bleedin' nuttin'.
HAIROIL	The rosser's are lagging Hatchet, Missus B.
MRS B.	(*running over*) Here, let him go.
1st P. MAN	It's none of your business, Missus.
MRS B.	What do yis think yis are doing with my son?
2nd P. MAN	(*showing razor*) He's in trouble, he had this.

49

MRS B.	Sure that's mine, he was collecting it for me.
HAIROIL	Correct.
FREDDIE	Ye were told he done nuttin'.
1st P. MAN	And where was be bringing it from?
MRS B.	Me sister in Credden Street.
2nd P. MAN	And what would you be doing with that thing?
MRS B.	I use it for cutting out the colours.
1st P. MAN	At this time of night?
MRS B.	Yis, he's a shift worker, aren't ye Brendan?
HATCHET	Yeah.
2nd P. MAN	(*handing razor to Mrs B.*) We'll let it go this time.
FREDDIE	You've no bleedin' choice pal.
1st P. MAN	What's your name? (*to* FREDDIE)
2nd P. MAN	And you funny fella? (*to* HAIROIL).
FREDDIE	Guess?

HAIROIL *giggles.*

1st P. MAN	We'll remember you.
2nd P. MAN	Now Missus, you bring that straight home, and look after it yourself in future. (*to* HATCHET) If I find you with anything like that again, you'll be for it.
1st P. MAN	So watch yourself. (*as* POLICEMEN *are exiting*).

POLICEMEN *are almost offstage when* FREDDIE *calls them.*

FREDDIE	Here, (POLICEMEN *turn*) I'll sing yis a song and it's not very long, All coppers is bastards.
2nd P. MAN	Take my advice and go home now before ye get into trouble.
1st P. MAN	You had better not be here when we get back.

TWO POLICEMEN *exit left wing.*

MRS B.	Are ye alright, Hatchet?
HATCHET	Yeah, it's late, go on home.
HAIROIL	We were lucky not to get done.
FREDDIE	We should have jumped them they were scared.
HATCHET	(*taking razor off Mrs B.*) Gimme that, and you better get out of here.
MRS B.	Don't be ordering me around now.

BRIDIE	Are ye coming, Hatchet?
HATCHET	Go on home, Bridie.
BRIDIE	Come with me.
ANGELA	You're wasting your time.
HATCHET	Go on, go on.
BRIDIE	What are you staying here for?
HATCHET	Will ye go home?
BRIDIE	I'm waiting on you.
ANGELA	He'll never change.
HATCHET	Get bleedin' going Bridie, and don't be annoying me.
MRS B.	Did they rough ye up, son?
BRIDIE	You'll only get into trouble out here.
HATCHET	Leave me a bleedin' lone and go off with your sister.
JOEY	I'll escort you, Ladies.
ANGELA	It's no use, Bridie, we'll leave ye home, (*to* HAIROIL) and that's where you should be as well, think of your wife and family.
HAIROIL	I am, why d'ye think I'm out bleedin' here?
JOEY	C'mon, Bridie, you'll be better off at home.
BRIDIE	Don't stay out long, Hatchet.
HA HA	(*slapping leg*) Well limbs, yis brought me here, now bring me home, c'mon left leg, wake yourself up, let's go, (*walking*) that's better.
JOEY	C'mon girls, it's been a night and a half.

JOEY, ANGELA, BRIDIE *and* HA HA *exit into left wing.*
HAIROIL *peers down lane.*

HATCHET	What are ye hanging around here for?
MRS B.	Don't be telling me what to do now.
HAIROIL	He's coming.
HATCHET	Mulally? (*peers into lane*).
MRS B.	Dog's vomit.
HATCHET	Shut up you, he looks drunk.
FREDDIE	Bleedin' destroy him.
HAIROIL	Don't hesitate, I'm with ye, Hatchet.
HATCHET	Wait till he gets down, see if he's gargled.
FREDDIE	Makes no difference, pal, he's a bleedin' goner.

MULALLY *arrives at end of laneway getting sick in corner.*

HAIROIL	Get the bastard.

FREDDIE	Kick his head in.
MRS B.	At last, ha ha.
HATCHET	Hold on, hold on a minute.
FREDDIE	Let him have it, Pal.
HAIROIL	He wouldn't give you a chance.
FREDDIE	Gimme me razor.
MRS B.	Watch the saw, son.
HATCHET	He's bleedin' drunk.
FREDDIE	So what, gimme it. (*snatches razor*).
HAIROIL	Don't be slow, Hatchet.
FREDDIE	I'll bleedin' get him. (*brandishing razor*).
HATCHET	(*holding* FREDDIE) No ye won't, get back.

MRS B. *takes off shoe running at* MULALLY *striking him.*

MRS B. Well I bleedin' will, ye bastard, ye dirty bastard.

HATCHET *pulls* MRS B. *off* MULALLY.

HATCHET Mother, for Jaysus' sake, mother.

HAIROIL *and* FREDDIE *descend on* MULALLY, *kicking and hitting him,* FREDDIE *uses the razor.*

HATCHET (*stopping attack*) O.K. He's enough, leave him, enough.

Attack stops, all look down on MULALLY, MRS B. *laughs.*

MRS B.	(*singing*) We got Mulally.
HATCHET	(*shoving* MRS B.) Shut bleedin' up, and walk straight, will ye.
MRS B.	(*singing*) My, my, my Mullally.
HATCHET	Right, we got him, and don't come crying to me again, d'ye hear? (*pushing her*) Get bleedin' going.
MRS B.	Why, why, why, Mulally. (*as they are walking off left*).

FREDDIE *and* HAIROIL *join in in low tones as they ex*

CURTAIN

END OF ACT TWO

Scene: The Bailey household and back lane.

Time: 10 a.m. approximately the next day.

When the curtain rises we see HATCHET *and* BRIDIE *at Pigeon Loft,*
HATCHET *is examining dead bird.*

BRIDIE	Is she really dead?
HATCHET	As a door nail.
BRIDIE	And I was looking forward to going to Belfast.
HATCHET	That's the way it goes, anyway I'm not so keen on it now.
BRIDIE	Hmm ... something happened last night ... yis got Mulally didn't yis?
HATCHET	He deserved it.
BRIDIE	I knew it ... that mother of yours ... she's no use.
HATCHET	(*throwing away dead bird*) Forget about it.

They walk towards house.

BRIDIE	I'm sorry to say it, but it's true, she causes nuttin' but trouble.

They enter house.

HATCHET	Is that right?
BRIDIE	I mean it, Hatchet.
HATCHET	Alright, ye mean it.
BRIDIE	Well, doesn't she?
HATCHET	Right, so she does.
BRIDIE	Could never be at peace, no one could settle down with that carry on.
HATCHET	Ah, relax outa that.
BRIDIE	I'm not used to that business, she's just no bloody use, that's all.
HATCHET	O.K. she's no use, fair enough. Either are you but, are ye?
BRIDIE	What?
HATCHET	Either are you but, are ye? You're afta been slagging me Ma about how useless she is. Well you're not much bleedin' better to me.

BRIDIE	What d'ye mean? I never get ye into rows or anything.
HATCHET	No, but ye don't give me much reason to bleedin' stay away from them. Jaysus, some wife you are.
BRIDIE	I look after ye, don't I?
HATCHET	Look after me? You're only a bleedin' housekeeper to me, that's all.
BRIDIE	I'm no housekeeper, Hatchet.
HATCHET	HAH!
BRIDIE	Don't be like that, Hatchet please, I don't like it.
HATCHET	(*in disgust*) Yahh!
BRIDIE	Maybe we haven't much, but at least we don't hate eachother. I don't want to argue, Hatchet, we'll only turn against each other, and we'll have nuttin' at all.
HATCHET	We have nuttin' now, nuttin', nuttin', nuttin', ye turned sour on me, I may as well be in bed with a bleedin' brush.
BRIDIE	I didn't.
HATCHET	Ye did, DID. Ye draw away from me. I don't know what to make of ye. D'ye not like kids or something?
BRIDIE	Don't be silly.
HATCHET	There's something wrong with you, d'ye know that?
BRIDIE	Oh no, there's not.
HATCHET	No? Well you're not mad about having kids, are ye?
BRIDIE	We're only married a year . . . I mean, give it time, and everything that should happen . . . er, probably will.
HATCHET	Give it time, are ye joking me? Ye hardly let me near ye. If you get pregnant there'll be three wise men from the east knocking at the door.
BRIDIE	Ye don't understand or know how I feel.
HATCHET	Little bleedin' Freddie going around with four kids. Huh, I don't know what sort of woman ye are. Ye want to see a doctor or something, Bridie, I'm telling ye.
BRIDIE	Don't be saying things like that to me.
HATCHET	You're bleedin' weird, you are.
BRIDIE	Don't say that.
HATCHET	What d'ye want me to bleedin' say?
BRIDIE	Alright, so I kept away from ye as often as possible, although I didn't want to. I swear to God I never did. And ye had your way with me when I thought it might be safe, when I was sure nuttin' could happen.

HATCHET   I bleedin' knew that. I knew it.
BRIDIE   Didn't want a baby . . . not yet, and I prayed to God it wouldn't happen, I did.
HATCHET   Why, Jaysus, why?
BRIDIE   I was afraid if we had one, we'd never get out of here, this bloody place.
HATCHET   What are ye on about?
BRIDIE   What d'ye think? We'd have been tied down here, never get away. And what if it was a boy? He'd never have a chance.
HATCHET   Don't talk stupid.
BRIDIE   That's the truth, Hatchet, he'd be hard and angry. He'd have to be. Be in trouble as soon as he was off the bottle, and with your mother to help him be like his famous grandfather "The Digger" or some other hardchaw.
HATCHET   Like me ye mean. Jaysus, you don't think much of me, do ye? Tell me . . . why did ye bleedin' marry me?
BRIDIE   I loved ye, Hatchet.
HATCHET   I don't understand, I swear I don't.
BRIDIE   I DID love ye, but I don't think I REALLY liked ye—the way ye went on sometimes. Only I was too full of ye then to realise it.
HATCHET   That's great, that's bleedin' great. Bridie yiv . . . I don't know, I thought we could've made a go of it, I mean ye knew me long enough before we got married.
BRIDIE   I know. And we could've. But not here, not here. Asked ye to move often enough . . . I have needs too, don't forget, . . . let's leave, Hatchet, let's go way.
HATCHET   Leave, just like that? Bridie, Bridie.
BRIDIE   It'll never be any use here.
HATCHET   And where are we supposed to bleedin' go?
BRIDIE   (standing up) Joey said he'll fix us up.
HATCHET   Ye can't just go way like that.
BRIDIE   D'ye love me, ye used to I know.
HATCHET   What are ye asking things like that for?
BRIDIE   I have to know, Hatchet.
HATCHET   Tch, I changed your name at the altar, didn't I? That should be your answer.
BRIDIE   (coming behind HATCHET) Well just ask Joey, will ye? No harm in just asking him, is there?

55

HATCHET	We'll see when he comes in.
BRIDIE	Promise me, say ye swear ye will.
HATCHET	I said I'll see him when he comes in, didn't I?
BRIDIE	And we'll go if he sez O.K.?
HATCHET	I suppose so.
BRIDIE	Make it definite, Hatchet, will ye?
HATCHET	If everything's alright, we'll go, deffo.
BRIDIE	Oh Hatchet, no more waking up and hating it.
HATCHET	It hasn't been all that bad.
BRIDIE	We'll be ourselves and live every day as it comes. I was going maudlin' here, . . . d'ye know what I done in the chapel last week?
HATCHET	What?
BRIDIE	The kids were making their communion. All the girls in white and their mothers fussing fixing their little veils . . . something came over me, I wanted to run some where and cry. Hatchet, couldn't do anything in this house. Couldn't even dream. (*pause*) I'll get ye some tea.
HATCHET	Tea? I'm sick drinking tea.
BRIDIE	Well have something to eat, eggs and rashers.
HATCHET	After all that gargle last night?
BRIDIE	Ah go on, I'll scramble them on toast, the way ye like them.
HATCHET	Bridie, it's a pint I want. Nourishment not punishment.

Enter HA HA *from door to hall carrying a shopping bag.*

BRIDIE	Ah, Ha Ha, c'mere, sit down. (*Sits him on sofa, fixes tie, combs hair etc.*) D'ye want a cup of tea, or will I give ye a bottle, or maybe I'll bring ye away with me?
HA HA	I have to get the messages.
BRIDIE	Bye and bye.
HA HA	Aha, aha lullaby.
BRIDIE	Yis Ha Ha (*sings*)

Well I had a little teddy,
And he wasn't very steady,
So I put him in the window for a show,
He fell out the window.
And he broke his little finger,
And he couldn't play his oul banjo,

He had no hair on the top of his head,
And he had no eyes to see.

HATCHET   You're going around the bend.

Enter JOEY *from door to hall.*

BRIDIE   Ah good morning, Joey.

JOEY   Morning, Bridie, how's Hatchet?

HATCHET   How are ye?

BRIDIE   Sit down, Joey, and have some tea. (JOEY *sits*) Did ye have your breakfast?

JOEY   I did.

BRIDIE   Are ye sure? I'm not bad with eggs.

HATCHET   Will ye leave the man alone?

BRIDIE   What ever ye say, boss.

JOEY   You're in great form this morning.

HATCHET   She's mad.

BRIDIE   Course I am, I married him.

BRIDIE *enters kitchen.*

HATCHET   Women.

JOEY   Yis, sure we can't live with them and we can't live without them, where's Nellie?

HATCHET   She's not down yet, will I give her a shout?

JOEY   No, sure she needs the rest.

HA HA   Messages, messages.

JOEY   (*hands* HA HA *money*) Get yourself some sweets, Ha Ha.

Enter BRIDIE *with tea tray, places tray on table.*

BRIDIE   Help yourself, Joey, (*examines list*) now everything's on the list, including the bones for me lord and master.

BRIDIE *puts list in* HA HA'S *pocket.*

HA HA   Ha ha sweets.

HA HA *exits door to hall.*

BRIDIE   Did ye ask him?

HATCHET	Not yet, give us a chance.
BRIDIE	Well go on, he won't bite ye, he had his breakfast, didn't ye Joey?
JOEY	Ask me what?
HATCHET	Well remember ye said ye could fix me up with a job?
JOEY	I do, of course.
HATCHET	Does it still stand?
JOEY	Er yes, you're thinking of going then?
HATCHET	Yeah, how soon could ye get me a start?
JOEY	As soon as ye like, they're always short of men.
BRIDIE	When are ye going back, Joey?
JOEY	Next Saturday.
BRIDIE	Can we go back with ye?
JOEY	Er why not, if you're ready in time?
BRIDIE	Right Hatchet? (HATCHET *is hesitant*) Alright?
HATCHET	O.K. I'll give in me notice on Monday.
JOEY	If yis don't mind me saying so, yis are going very sudden.
BRIDIE	Our minds are made up, Joey.
JOEY	I'm not trying to put yis off now, but it isn't everyone that likes it over there, ye know?
HATCHET	We'll be alright.
JOEY	Many's the time I regretted going away meself.
BRIDIE	Sure ye wouldn't've got on if ye stayed here.
JOEY	That's true, but ah, it does something to ye. They're different over there and ye have to change like, and when ye come home ye feel strange with your own.
HATCHET	It won't bother me. I just hope you like it.
BRIDIE	I'll like it. I don't care what it's like. Sure can't we always come back in a few years and get our own home. Joey said the money was good.
JOEY	True enough and there's plenty of overtime.
HATCHET	Right, that's it so.
JOEY	Nellie won't like it.
HATCHET	Can't do anything about that.
BRIDIE	We're going? We're really going?
HATCHET	We'll give it a try.

BRIDIE *kisses* HATCHET *on cheek.*

HATCHET	Stop messing will ye? (BRIDIE *continues to pet* HATCHET).

BRIDIE *is laughing with joy as* TWO POLICEMEN *enter briskly, from door to hall.*

1st P. MAN	Get your coat, Bailey.
HATCHET	What?
2nd P. MAN	C'mon, you're coming with us.
1st P. MAN	And no nonsense like last night.
JOEY	Ah now, hold on a minute.
2nd P. MAN	Who are you?
JOEY	A friend of the family.

Enter MRS B. *from door to hall.*

MRS B.	What's up, what do yous want here?
1st P. MAN	You know well enough. This bloody son of yours . . .
MRS B.	Mind your language, watch your tongue now.
HATCHET	What are ye talking about?
2nd P. MAN	You'll find out, you're for it this time.
HATCHET	Ye what?
1st P. MAN	You should have gone home like we told ye last night.
2nd P. MAN	Bloody hardman, we'd be in bed now only for you.
HATCHET	What are yis getting at?
1st P. MAN	Don't give us that. Didn't ye act the hardchaw around the laneway last night?
HATCHET	Hold on, I wasn't hanging around anywhere. I came straight home, didn't I Ma?
MRS B.	That's exactly right.
BRIDIE	Yis he did.
2nd P. MAN	Didn't ye have it in for someone, Bailey?
HATCHET	No I didn't, no.
1st P. MAN	You had better be able to prove that.
HATCHET	Wasn't I with me mates, and me family was there as well.
MRS B.	He's plenty of witnesses, what do you want to know for?
2nd P. MAN	A man from around here, Mulally, was attacked in the laneway last night, and seriously injured.
HATCHET	What's that got to do with me?
1st P. MAN	We know you were involved in it.
HATCHET	You're mistaken.
2nd P. MAN	You were there alright.
HATCHET	Not me, I don't go in for that caper anymore.

1st P. MAN	Didn't ye give us trouble there last night?
HATCHET	You gave us trouble. I was only waiting on me mother. I know nuttin' about Mulally.
MRS B.	He didn't do it. Why don't ye ask Mulally who done it?
2nd P. MAN	We will, when he can talk. They had to cut open his windpipe, there was something caught in it.
1st P. MAN	He's lucky to be alive, but he'll tell us who done it when he's better.
2nd P. MAN	Mulally will talk Bailey, he'll talk.
1st P. MAN	The best thing ye can do is to own up, it'll be easier on you in the long run.
HATCHET	I already told ye. I didn't do anything.

TWO POLICEMEN *approach* HATCHET, HATCHET *backs off.*

2nd P. MAN	You had better come with us and make a statement.
HATCHET	I'm making no statement.
1st P. MAN	You're coming with us anyway.
HATCHET	That's what you bleedin' think.

HATCHET *dashes out back door.*

2nd P. MAN	After him.
1st P. MAN	We'll get ye, Bailey.

TWO POLICEMEN *follow* HATCHET *out back door.*

MRS B.	Ha ha, Hatchet'll give them a run for their money.
BRIDIE	But what's going to happen to us, Missus.
JOEY	Don't worry, Bridie.
MRS B.	Nuttin' will happen, the policemen's feet will just get flatter, that's all.
BRIDIE	But if they get him?
MRS B.	Let them, they can't prove anything. (*sits chair top left*).
BRIDIE	What if Mulally squeals to the police?
JOEY	A bad pill that.
MRS B.	Mulally wouldn't talk to them. He wouldn't be able to show his face around here again if he did.
BRIDIE	But he might, ye heard the policeman.
MRS B.	For God's sake, I told ye he won't. He couldn't even if he wanted to—he was too drunk. You're an awful

	woman, Bridie.
BRIDIE	Please God nuttin' will happen to him.

Enter FREDDIE *and* HAIROIL *from door to hall.*

JOEY	Ah, the boys themselves.
HAIROIL	We saw the law moving out, what's up?
BRIDIE	The police are after Hatchet.
MRS B.	Yis, over Mulally. Now if they question ye, yis know nuttin', d'ye hear?
HAIROIL	Are ye joking me?
FREDDIE	They'll get bleedin' nuttin' out of me.
BRIDIE	Do yis realise what happened Mulally?
FREDDIE	What's it matter?
HAIROIL	Hatchet'll get away with it, Bridie.
BRIDIE	HE nearly died the policeman said.
FREDDIE	I gave him a right boot.
HAIROIL	What about the digs I landed?
FREDDIE	And I gave him a very close bleedin' shave.
MRS B.	Serves him right.
JOEY	Very serious offence.
BRIDIE	How serious?
JOEY	Eight . . . ten years.
FREDDIE	If they get ye.
HAIROIL	And if they have a witness.
MRS B.	Which they haven't.
FREDDIE	And if the witness can talk.
HAIROIL	Which he can't.
MRS B.	So ye see?
BRIDIE	It would kill Hatchet, he hates being kept in.
HAIROIL	Now, Bridie, he'd be among friends.
BRIDIE	Friends!
FREDDIE	Sure, I was brought up on porridge.
HAIROIL	Mountjoy brand.
FREDDIE	Hard porridge, pal.
HAIROIL	Stirwell before using, he, he, he.
BRIDIE	Yous two are crazy.
FREDDIE	Stir crazy, ha, ha, ha.

FREDDIE *and* HAIROIL *are laughing insanely when*
JOHNNYBOY MULALLY *and two young men enter from
door to hall.*

MRS B.	Who are yous, who d'ye think ye are bursting in here?
JOHNNYBOY	Shut your mouth, ye oul cow. Is any of these him?
1st MAN	No, Johnnyboy.
JOHNNYBOY	Check the rooms.

1st MAN *checks upstairs,* 2nd MAN *kitchen and yard.*

MRS B.	What d'ye think you're doing?
JOHNNYBOY	Shut bleedin' up or I'll shut ye up, who are you?
MRS B.	Mrs Bailey, if it's any of your business.
JOHNNYBOY	Mrs bleedin' Bailey, it's business of mine alright, you're son is called Hatchet right?
MRS B.	What about it?

The two men re-enter living room.

1st MAN	No one there, Johnnyboy.
2nd MAN	No sign of him.
JOHNNYBOY	When I get him I'm going to cut his head off (*suddenly displays a large knife*) I'm going to carve your bleedin' son up. Who are yous?
BRIDIE	They're just friends.
JOHNNYBOY	Ye know my brother?
HAIROIL	Yeah sure.
FREDDIE	Seen him around.
JOHNNYBOY	Well he was jumped on last night by a few bastards. The Hatchet fella was one. Yous are mates of his, are'n't yis?
HAIROIL	Ye could say that.
FREDDIE	We hang around together.
JOHNNYBOY	Were yis with him last night? (*neither reply*) Were yis bleedin' with him?
HAIROIL	Er what?
FREDDIE	What's this about?
MRS B.	So you're a Mulally, I should've known by your big nose. Don't worry, Hatchet done him on his own. It was easy, he didn't need anyone. And he won't need anyone for you either.
JOHNNYBOY	Ye poxy oul cow, I told ye to shut up (*approaching* MRS B.).
MRS B.	Don't call me names, ye ignorant pig.

JOEY *gets between* JOHNNYBOY *and* MRS B.

JOHNNYBOY Get out of me bleedin' way you, QUICK!

JOEY Ah now, she's a woman, remember that, she's a woman.

JOHNNYBOY You're lucky I'm not after you, ye stupid oul bastard. Remember that. You ever do that and I'll cut your bleedin' throat, (*to Bridie*) you, when is he coming back?

BRIDIE I don't know, why don't ye leave us alone?

JOHNNYBOY I'll leave yis alone alright, the way my brother was left. You tell your man—Johnnyboy Mulally was here. And tell him to get that hatchet of his, because I'm coming back, (*waves knife*) and I have this for him, and you, his oulwan, you won't know your son when I'm finished with him. I'll take his bleedin' life, I will.

MRS B. Go way, ye jailbird, ye should be locked away.

JOHNNYBOY I just done seven over a bloke, ye oul bag. Another stretch won't bother me—as long as I get that bastarding son of yours. That's all that matters, that swine. (*to* HAIROIL *and* FREDDIE) And you two, I won't forget yous either. Ye know where they live?

1st MAN Down the road.

JOHNNYBOY Right, and I know your bleedin' faces. If I find out yis had anything to do with last night I'll cut yis bleedin' up, right? C'mon.

JOHNNYBOY *and two men exit door to hall.*

BRIDIE God, where's it all going to end, police and all coming to the door.

MRS B. Ah shut up, Bridie, police and trouble are all the one around here, same difference.

BRIDIE And that man, he's terrible.

MRS B. (*to* FREDDIE *and* HAIROIL) See if yous can find Hatchet.

BRIDIE Before Mulally does . . . he's an animal.

FREDDIE Right, pal, c'mon.

MRS B. He'll be sorry he set foot in this house, I'm telling ye.

HAIROIL Too true, Mrs B., too true.

HAIROIL *and* FREDDIE *exit door to hall.*

63

BRIDIE	Thank God we're going away.
MRS B.	What?
BRIDIE	Thank God we're going away I said. Me and Hatchet are going away.
MRS B.	When did all this happen?
BRIDIE	This morning, we asked Joey. All the arrangements are made.
JOEY	Yeah . . . they want to go back with me, Nell.
MRS B.	Oh, ah don't mind the Mulallys, Bridie, that'll blow over.
BRIDIE	We're not staying here and it's not just the Mulallys. Our mind's made up. We're going with Joey.
MRS B.	Hatchet asked ye?
JOEY	He talked about it Nellie.
BRIDIE	Yis he did.
MRS B.	He asked ye?
JOEY	Yis Nell, this morning.
BRIDIE	I told ye so.
MRS B.	And yis are going back with him?
BRIDIE	As soon as we can.
JOEY	I couldn't very well talk him out of it, Nell.
MRS B.	Well, well, . . . I suppose yis know what yis want, yis are old enough anyway. Life is full of surprises. 1970 was a big surprise for Nellie. A whole year a widow. And now me son . . . Hatchet . . . me son. Ah well the best of luck to yis. Me and Ha Ha will make out . . . where is he?
BRIDIE	Gone for the messages.

Enter ANGELA *from door to hall.*

MRS B.	And what do you want?
ANGELA	I'm seeing me sister, what's the commotion?
BRIDIE	The police want Hatchet over Mulally.
ANGELA	I heard about it. His brother and two other ruffians are at the corner.
BRIDIE	They were in here, Angela, here. They're after him, I don't know what's going to happen.
ANGELA	Something like that was bound to happen with all that hardchaw carry on.
MRS B.	Ah shut your trap, we've enough on our plate without you.
ANGELA	I knew he'd drag ye into something like this, knew it.

JOEY	That Johnnyboy is really vicious. Cares about no one.
ANGELA	Keep out of it Bridie, come down to my place.
JOEY	Do that Bridie, it could get very rough here.
BRIDIE	No, I'm staying.
JOEY	If it comes to the push that Johnnyboy will break in, and he'll cut down anyone in his way, woman or no woman.
MRS B.	Bad cess on him, now Bridie, ye see what you're up against. Ye didn't see Mulally coming in on his knees, did ye?
JOEY	Go with your sister, Bridie, that's the best thing, tell her Nellie.
MRS B.	I'll tell her nuttin'. Nuttin'. She doesn't need me to tell her what to do.
ANGELA	C'mon Bridie, you'd be better off outa here.
BRIDIE	I'm not leaving.
ANGELA	Ye heard him—that gangster will break in.
BRIDIE	I'm waiting on Hatchet.
MRS B.	Let them come. I've seen it all before. It won't be the first time I've used a bottle, and my Jaysus I'll use it on them.

BRIDIE *starts to clear table.*

ANGELA	Bridie c'mon, me mother didn't rear ye for this.
MRS B.	Stuff you and your mother. No one asked ye to come, and leave the table alone Bridie.
JOEY	Now girls.
BRIDIE	I may as well do SOMETHING.
MRS B.	Leave it alone I said. It's my house. I'll look after it.
JOEY	Relax Bridie.
BRIDIE	RELAX?
MRS B.	Don't strain yourself. Save your energy for your own place. You'll need your strength for when ye go way.
ANGELA	Go way? . . . Who?
MRS B.	Ah did ye not know? Yis, your little sister is going away with Hatchet.
ANGELA	When?
BRIDIE	Next Monday.
ANGELA	The two of yis?
BRIDIE	I'm his wife, aren't I?
ANGELA	That's very sudden, Bridie.
MRS B.	Isn't it now? She can't get away quick enough.

You'd think I had leprosy or something.

ANGELA Why is he going?

MRS B. How would I know? I'm only his mother.

JOEY Ye never know, it might be for the best, what d'ye think, Nell?

MRS B. The best?

JOEY Well ye never know.

HAIROIL *pokes head around door to hall.*

HAIROIL Any sign of your man?

MRS B. D'ye see him, Hairoil, are ye going blind as well as baldy?

HAIROIL Thought he might have sneaked back in.

FREDDIE, *who is keeping a watchful eye on events in the street, enters abruptly from door to hall.*

FREDDIE He was seen coming out of the shipping office.

FREDDIE *exits as quickly as he enters.*

BRIDIE Tickets.

MRS B. What tickets?

JOEY Boat tickets.

MRS B. Jaysus! Well find him before that tribe does.

HAIROIL They're still at the corner, Missus B.

BRIDIE Joey will you see what ye can do?

JOEY Er . . . certainly.

HAIROIL Right, c'mon pal.

BRIDIE Don't bring him back if they're still out there.

JOEY Not to worry, he'll be alright.

MRS B. Don't be wasting time, go on, will yis?

JOEY Don't fret, Nell, we'll find him.

JOEY *and* HAIROIL *exit door to hall.*

BRIDIE What if they catch him on his own, there's three of them and that fella has the knife. They'll cut him to bits, he won't have a chance.

MRS B. Hatchet can take care of himself.

ANGELA Himself, he's not worrying about Bridie.

BRIDIE Even if the police don't get him it's no use, not with

	them hooligans out there. Where's it all going to end?
ANGELA	Ye should've left him long ago.
BRIDIE	Wish I could do something.
MRS B.	You'll get used to it, same as I did. Many's the wait I've had. Too many. Waiting and wondering if he was alright. Ah but he was worth waiting for. Was. Was. I'd do it all over again, black eyes and all.
BRIDIE	That's alright for you, what if he goes to prison?
MRS B.	You'll get used to that too. One visit a month. 20 minutes only. Don't pass anything to the prisoner. No touching. No whispering. No kissing. Section 4, Rule 6, bleedin' prison regulations. Allowed one letter a month, that's if your husband can read. Mine couldn't even spell his name. So ye hang on for that 20 minutes every month hoping he'll get out early for good behaviour. And when he does he'll probably beat ye black and blue because he just won't believe that your were on your good behaviour as well . . . ah yiv a lot to learn yet, woman.
ANGELA	Lots that she's better off not knowing, Missus.
MRS B.	It's all life, isn't it?
ANGELA	Not for our family.
MRS B.	Your family. A clean shirt every Sunday—and not an arse in their trousers for the rest of the week.
BRIDIE	Oh don't start again.

Enter JOEY, HATCHET, FREDDIE *and* HAIROIL *from door to hall.* HATCHET *carries a bag of beer.* (*Bottles and cans*).

JOEY	We found him down the road.

HATCHET *sits chair bottom right of table,* HAIROIL *sits chair top right.* JOEY *sits on sofa.* FREDDIE *lounges back wall.*

HATCHET	(*putting beer on table*) Hello Ma, hello Bridie, (*to* ANGELA) Ah hello beaky, after the free dinners again, are ye?
ANGELA	I am not, the cheek of you. I didn't come here to be insulted.
HATCHET	Well get out then.
ANGELA	I beg your pardon!

HATCHET	Go on, get bleedin' out.
ANGELA	I only came here for my sister. Bridie, are you coming?
BRIDIE	Leave me alone, Angela.
ANGELA	I'm going, and if you've any sense you'll get away from that . . . that savage right away.
HATCHET	Bye, bye, say hello to the coppers for me.
ANGELA	(*at door to hall*) Say hello yourself—you'll be seeing them soon enough.
HATCHET	Only if they're emigrating.

Derisive gestures and hoots of laughter from FREDDIE, HAIROIL.

ANGELA	(*exiting*) Animals!
BRIDIE	They won't stop till they find ye, Hatchet.
HATCHET	They'll never make it stick.
BRIDIE	Ye won't go to prison?
HATCHET	No, sure they're only after me because they found Mulally. I'll get away with it alright.
FREDDIE	Snake swines.
BRIDIE	Are ye sure, Hatchet?
HATCHET	Yeah, it won't affect us, Bridie. By the way, did she tell ye, Ma? We're going away.
MRS B.	She told me alright.
HAIROIL	Miss ye mate.
HATCHET	You'll be O.K., won't ye?
MRS B.	Course I will. Ye could've told me yourself but, Hatchet. Wouldn't've said anything. I wouldn't hold ye back from something ye really wanted to do.
HATCHET	It's one of those things that happen, Ma. Anyway, you won't go short. I'll send ye a few bob every week.
FREDDIE	Good money in England, pal.
MRS B.	Drop a line now and then, if ye like. Doesn't really matter what ye say in it.
HATCHET	Ye can be sure of that, Ma.
BRIDIE	We'll write every week, Mrs Bailey.
MRS B.	Do that. Won't answer it meself but. No use at making up letters.
BRIDIE	That won't matter.
MRS B.	The woman next door will write for me. She's very good at them things. Her first husband was a clerk in the corporation.
HATCHET	Sure Ma, yeah.

There is a long pause before MRS BAILEY *replies. It is almost as if the Irish Sea is already between them.*

MRS B.   Yeah.

FREDDIE   Go with ye, buddy, only the English police always send me back to Dublin on the next boat.

HAIROIL   Same here, I've a record over there as well.

FREDDIE   Feel like a bleedin' yo yo sometimes, I do.

HATCHET   Right, well let's have a drink. (*takes beer out of bag*).

MRS B.   Celebrate son, go on, did yis not tell him what happened?

JOEY   We told him, Nellie.

MRS B.   Johnnyboy Mulally was here, waving a knife and threatening everybody.

HATCHET   I know all about it, Ma.

BRIDIE   He's out to get ye, Hatchet.

HATCHET   So I believe. Anyone for a drink? No. Smoke then? No? Fair enough. (*lights cigarette, drinks beer*).

BRIDIE   This is serious, Hatchet.

JOEY   Listen, son.

HAIROIL   Johnnyboy's a lot different to his brother.

MRS B.   He's bigger, that's all, and he's got a mouth to go with it.

FREDDIE   He's a dangerous bleeder.

MRS B.   It won't be the first time ye had to stand up for yourself, and don't think I'll let ye face them on your own.

BRIDIE   A big knife he has, he said he's going to use it on ye.

FREDDIE   That's if he gets the bleedin' chance.

BRIDIE   He's determined to hurt ye, he's bad, bad.

MRS B.   Hatchet could hurt him too, don't forget that.

HATCHET   Or I could hurt him too, don't forget that. Ma, I bleedin' knew it. I knew you'd say something like that. Ah well, it's not a bad morning and it might pick up, what?

MRS B.   What are ye talking about, is he drunk or what, Joey?

JOEY   I er . . . a few.

HATCHET   A couple I had, that's all. Now don't be getting steamed up about it.

BRIDIE   Did Mulally see yis coming in?

FREDDIE   They weren't there.

HAIROIL   Ye want to get ready for him, Hatchet.

BRIDIE   You'll have to keep away from him, he's in a terrible

	temper.
JOEY	Terrible.
HATCHET	He's not, is he, I wonder why? It couldn't be over his brother, could it? I mean we only bleedin' milled him when he was dead drunk, that's all.
MRS B.	He deserved it.
FREDDIE	Should've bleedin' killed him.
HATCHET	And we kicked his head in, as well as a few digs. True he's alive. Well he's still breathing even if it is through a hole in his neck.
MRS B.	Stop playing around. Somethings' got to be done. Ye better have your mind made up before that swine comes back.
HATCHET	Is that right? Well right now I'm enjoying this drink. That's all I know and it's all I want to know.
MRS B.	Don't be acting the fool. He came in here and terrorised the place. He even threatened to do Joey.
JOEY	Don't mind me, Hatchet.
HATCHET	I'm not minding ye at all, Joey.
MRS B.	You'd better do something.
HATCHET	Do something like bleedin' what?
MRS B.	What do you think?
BRIDIE	Do nothing, we're going away.
HAIROIL	Go after him.
FREDDIE	I can get a team, Hatchet.
HAIROIL	Meet him somewhere away from the house.
HATCHET	And what then?
MRS B.	Do the bastard.
FREDDIE	It's the only way, pal.
JOEY	Don't rush into anything, lads.
HATCHET	Is that all ye want? Just do the bastard?
MRS B.	He's coming after you, isn't he?
HATCHET	Is he?
MRS B.	Course he is.
HATCHET	Well I don't want to do the bastard. I don't even know if he is a bastard, and I couldn't care less anyway.
MRS B.	And d'ye think Mulally is going to let by what happened last night?
HAIROIL	Never.
FREDDIE	Not Johnnyboy.
HATCHET	So what? Bridie and me are going away. I've got the tickets.

70

MRS B.	Tell him someone, will yis? He'll go for ye with the knife the minute he sees ye.
FREDDIE	If he gets ye without a weapon you're done for.
HAIROIL	You're dead duck without a tool, Hatchet.
MRS B.	Take the bottles away, Joey, he's enough.

JOEY *attemps to take bottles.*

HATCHET	Leave them there.
JOEY	(*desisting*) Take it easy, son.
BRIDIE	Don't get drunk, Hatchet, please, not at this time.
MRS B.	Ah you're lovely, the mess we're in and all you can do is drink.
HATCHET	D'ye play darts, Joey?
JOEY	Er. . . . yis, now and again.
HATCHET	Great, we'll have a few nights out together in England, what d'ye say?
JOEY	Oh, we could do that alright.
HATCHET	That's what I like, ye know that. A few gargles, a game of darts and me pigeons out there. That's all I want. That's me.
JOEY	Nuttin' wrong with that.
HATCHET	No . . . Ye know there's three boozers over there I can't go into. That's a fact. Not even for a chat, never mind a game. They won't serve me. Rows. I'm barred, bleedin' hardchaw.
MRS B.	Make black coffee for him, Bridie.
HATCHET	You're making nuttin' for me, Bridie, and will you shut up outa that?
JOEY	Take it, it'll do ye good.
HATCHET	Look, I'm not getting bleedin' drunk. Listen to this, Joey, will ye? A probation officer told me this.
FREDDIE	Probation officers is no bleedin' use.
HATCHET	A man went out to find his enemies, and he found no friends. Now, A man went out to find his friends, And he found no enemies, What d'ye think of that, Joey, d'ye get it?
JOEY	Yis, it's good right enough.
MRS B.	What's wrong with ye, Hatchet?
HATCHET	Too bleedin' true it's good, ye know the first part, "A man went out to find his enemies"?

JOEY	I remember yis.
HATCHET	Well that's bleedin' me, d'ye know that? The probation officer told me that years ago.
HAIROIL	That crowd would tell ye anything.
HATCHET	Looking for me enemies, getting into stupid rows over nuttin', that right Ma?
MRS B.	Don't be annoying me, you're making a show of yourself.
HATCHET	There ye are, Joey, I'm making a show of meself.
JOEY	Don't drink so much son.
MRS B.	Don't mind him, Joey.
HATCHET	Do I make a show of meself when I'm bashing someone's head in?
MRS B.	Shut up, shut up.
HATCHET	Oh no, or when I kicked someone in the face. That was standing up for meself, wasn't it?
MRS B.	I'm finished with you after this.
HATCHET	Do ye know how people will respect ye around here, Joey? By acting like a man. By standing up for yourself and if anyone looks sideways at ye—give him good kick in the knackers.
FREDDIE	Two kicks is bleedin' better.
HATCHET	And that's how everyone around here will respect ye. But they won't bleedin' like ye and that's a fact.
JOEY	I mind me own business, that's all I do.

Loud knocks are heard at door to hall.

BRIDIE	There's someone at the door.
HATCHET	Well?

Knocks are repeated.

HATCHET	Is someone going to bleedin' answer it? Alright I'll get it.
JOEY	(*rising*) I'll see who it is.

JOEY *exits door to hall—voices can be heard off-stage.*

JOHNNYBOY	Is he there?
JOEY	Who?
JOHNNYBOY	Don't give me that, ye oul bastard, is he fuckin there?
1st MAN	He was seen going in, Johnnyboy. (*shouting*).

72

JOHNNYBOY	Right, that swine to the laneway, I'll be bleedin' waiting. And if ye don't come out, Hatchetman, I'll burn this kip down and every whoring swine in it. D'ye hear me? Down the lane, Bailey. Me and you, ye bastard.

JOEY *enters from door to hall.*

JOEY	Ye heard him.
MRS B.	I told ye, ye wouldn't listen.
BRIDIE	Too late, it's too late now.
MRS B.	Is that all ye can say when they're going to burn my home?
BRIDIE	Oh mammy, Jaysus, Mary and Joseph.

JOHNNYBOY *and* TWO MEN *are now prancing up and and down lane.*

JOHNNYBOY	Come out, Hatchetman.
HATCHET	Yous two better get out of here.
FREDDIE	I can get a team and they carry tools. They'll sort them bleedin' out.
HAIROIL	It's the only way.
HATCHET	Ah get bleedin' lost the pair of ye.
MRS B.	Get them, go on, what are yis waiting for? Get them.
HAIROIL	They'll be sorry.
FREDDIE	We'll be back rapid, pal.

HAIROIL *and* FREDDIE *exit door to hall.*

JOHNNYBOY	C'mon Bailey, ye swine.
MRS B.	Jaysus, d'ye hear him, what's got into ye?
JOHNNYBOY	C'mon ye yellah pig, I'm waiting, I'm bleedin' waiting.
MRS B.	Don't let yourself down, Hatchet. Everyone will walk over ye now, everyone.
HATCHET	Just shut bleedin' up.
MRS B.	Jaysus, do something. What if he comes in? I'm alright, but what about Bridie?
BRIDIE	Leave him alone you.
MRS B.	What?
BRIDIE	Leave him alone, ye stupid woman. It's all over you anyway.

JOEY	Bridie, you're upset.
MRS B.	Don't you start, Bridie.
BRIDIE	Bloody woman, ye bloody woman ye.
JOEY	What's the use.
MRS B.	Ah you know nuttin'.
JOHNNYBOY	Come out ye bleedin' swine or I'll burn ye out.
MRS B.	(*shouting into lane*) Ah ye pox scarred get, who's your father, Mulally, who's your father?
JOHNNYBOY	Get that bastarding son of yours out here.
CHANT	HA HA HATCHET HA HA HA HA.
HATCHET	Ye don't bleedin' understand Ma, d'ye?
JOEY	(*picking up hat*) Still the same.
MRS B.	I don't care if he does do ye. Don't be afraid of him, the bleedin' bastard.
HATCHET	I can't explain it to ye, Ma, it's not that.
JOHNNYBOY	C'mon fuckin' Hatchetman.
CHANT	HA HA HATCHET HA HA HA HA HA HA.

Chant continues as HA HA *slowly enters from backyard. He has been brutally beaten. His face is lacerated.* BRIDIE *seats* HA HA *centre.*

MRS B.	Bastards, bastards, bastards.
BRIDIE	Poor Ha Ha.

JOEY *hands him can of beer.*

JOEY	Drink that, oul son.
HA HA	Ha ha.

MRS B. *takes bottle off fireplace and breaks it off table.*

MRS B.	I'm not standing for that. You can stay here if ye like. I'll do it for ye. The swine, the swines.
HATCHET	Ah you're not going out there, Ma, you're not.
MRS B.	I am, I bleedin' am.

JOEY *puts on hat walks to door to hall, turns around.*

JOEY	The best of luck . . . the lot of yis.

JOEY *exits.*

HATCHET	(*taking bottle off* MRS B.) Ah Jaysus come back, come bleedin' back, gimme that.
BRIDIE	Ye cow, ye bitch ye, you've ruined everything, everything.
HATCHET	Right Mulally, right Mulally bastard.
HA HA	(*thumping beer can against forehead*) Ha ha ha ha.
MRS B.	(*breaking another neck off bottle*) Ah no son, I'm not letting ye face them animals alone. I'll take the head off the first swine that comes near me.
BRIDIE	Ye bitch, ye bitch ye, ye dirty rotten, cowing, whoring, pigging bitch.
JOHNNYBOY	Come on fuckin' Hatchetman.
HA HA	HA ha ha ha haha.

HATCHET *goes to door to back yard followed by* MRS B.

MRS B.	Come on love. I'm with ye. C'mon chicken love.
HATCHET	Mulally ye scabby nosed bastard.
BRIDIE	Hatchet . . . I'm going with ye.

BRIDIE *runs after* HATCHET *and* MRS B.

Lights dimmed on all characters except HA HA, *who growls sub-humanly as he accelerates thumping his forehead with beer can until froth overflows.*

| HA HA | Haha, haha, haha, ha . . . hatchet (*Screams*) HATCHET! |

Lights out.

CURTAIN

END OF PLAY